I0586386

Hunter's Moon
CAGED
BOOK 4

By

V J GARLAND

V.J.Garland

Hunter's Moon: Caged

Caged Hunter's Moon Book #4 by V.J.Garland

Published by V.J.Garland

https://vanessajgarland.com/

Copyright © 2023 V.J.Garland

For permissions contact: vgarland89@outlook.com

Book Cover Illustration by Angie Liu
Editor: Joey Prosser

ISBN: 978-0-6487069-9-1
ISBN: 979-8-8608515-5-9

First Edition.

Genre: Thriller/Fantasy/Horror/Romance

Summary: The demise of the precinct saw the survival of the fittest fighting for their lives through new traumas, new people, and harder choices. The world is different, people are different, but so are they.

V.J.Garland

V.J.GARLAND

Hunter's
Moon

U.J.Garland

V.J.Garland

V.J.GARLAND

Hunter's Moon
THE PRECINCT

V.J.Garland

CHAPTER ONE

JAX

We raced as fast as we could to the river. Austin had Celinde on his back as he bounded in front of me. He dumped her into a single kayak, and she sprang into action thrashing around to look for a paddle. Austin leapt into the water and pushed her out as far as he could. Celinde began paddling with her arms when she was unable to find an ore, but she was weak, and she soon gave up and allowed Austin to push her through the shallows when she realized her efforts made no difference.

Liam and Ezra helped me with Carrie and Christian's bodies. Each went into a double kayak as one of us paddled but it was useless. Their corpses vanished into clouds of smoke within minutes and like always, we'd never be able to say a proper goodbye.

There was no way out of here alive. Guns fired at us from the cityscape and bridges as water vessels launched from the boat ramps. We were being hunted by humans *and* werewolves now. They fought one another as they both chased us down. Trucks full of humans with weapons were overturned by the new werewolves as the once caged wolves made their way through what was not so long ago their safe zone.

We barely made it to the memorial bridge before more humans got word of the crossfire and started dropping homemade bombs on everything in the water. The boats became engulfed with fire; the fuel erupting in explosions and soon enough the blowback hit us. We all dove from our kayaks and swam to the closest bank— but we weren't all on the same side of the river.

Celinde was on the opposite shoreline, as was Liam. He was almost two hundred feet away from here. Gunfire was heavy on our side of the river as more humans waged war to fight against us and the rouge werewolves.

"We need to help them!" Austin pleaded as he looked to Liam and Celinde alone on the other side and the sky darkened as explosions filled the air with smoke and debris rained down around us.

I agreed as I forced out my inner beast, Ezra did the same, quickly followed by Austin. It was never an easy transition through the day, I never felt right in this skin. My hands were still humanlike, my coloring never complete, but I was still superior and powerful.

It was no easy decision, the last time I killed my own kind I didn't think I'd survive, but what more did I have to live for. *Just don't get it in your mouth!* Something I hummed to myself like my life depended on it—but really, it did.

Ezra sprung into a pack of wolves, he gnashed his teeth fierce and violently and he tore flesh from bones and left wolves limbless and ready to be put down if they weren't already on the cusp of death. Austin bounded away next; Liam was crossing the river as I raced to hurl cars and motorbikes at the humans on the other side trying to shower him in bullets. Crash after thud they landed cutting off the humans advances on him.

It took both of us to have the power to collapse the bridge. We struck the cement thunderously with a force as hard as we could muster. Several attempts later and we had sunk it into the Gun Island Chute. As the debris fell it created a blockade in the water, the pieces of concrete connected with one another like a shambled tetris.

Celinde raced into the sparse trees as we began to raze the second bridge. Flames raged behind me as the trees became fuel to the blaze and engulfed our surroundings.

The smell of singed hair wafted over us and screams could be heard as wolves began to turn back into humans completely unaware their human form would slow any healing, they were better off as werewolves now.

We were outnumber, five to one at the very least. A hoard descended upon us. Newly born werewolves eager for the opportunity to feel their first fight and the chomping of their jaws echoed loudly. The hunger ignited the carnal instinct within them. I let out a howl, deep and piercing. It was unlike anything I'd ever heard *or* done. And it commanded one thing, obedience.

I stood taller than all of them and I let my height intimidate them as I began to pick them off from around my family. Some snarled, others snapped at me. The fire was pushing them closer, and the heat radiated in our direction.

I knew I had to hold them here just a little while longer if Celinde was going to stand any chance. She was alone, on foot and as far as I could tell there were no wolves on that side of the river.

These wolves were quickly agitated, embers flew up at them and hairs fizzled as they hesitated to move closer as Ezra, Austin and Liam defended the bank. I tore through trees and launched them like spears at any wolf moving too close—a trick I had learnt from Lupe.

But the wind was against us, and we were all about to be toast if we didn't run.

Liam was edgy after swimming over. He'd been hurt and was still in the phase of healing when a smaller wolf lunged for him as he noticed he was slightly more vulnerable than the rest of us. Ezra caught him before he hit Liam and tore him to the ground. He gorged himself on the body, leaving barely anything but bones as we all watched on in horror. He lifted his muzzle to reveal a bloodied face, and red eyes. I knew then and there this was the beginning of the end for Ezra.

His body became gluttonous as he scoured the group for more, his hunger dissatisfied with what it had just devoured.

Most of the wolves ran through the fire, desperately hoping to evade Ezra and escape with few burns. But the scent of that fire told us something different, it was a burnt barbeque full of werewolves and the few humans who weren't able to escape in time. The few who didn't run were scalded in burns and bite marks. Their healing abilities were still slow and not quite catching.

Ezra launched for the biggest one still amongst us. He had him down, fangs deep in his neck before I tore him off the body that was jerking as death stole it from his claws. Ezra was visibly distressed I'd cut his fun short and he thrashed around against me.

He arced up and threatened to fight me, likely more because he was interested in what I might taste like. Liam snatched the body and rolled it into the river as I tried to restrain Ezra. But Liam's attempt to diffuse the situation wasn't enough. The removal of the body or *food* just stirred an anger in Ezra as I threw him to the ground trying to stop him.

The other werewolves morphed back as they ran to the river and waited in the shallows as they watched curiously at what was happening between us.

Austin sat atop Ezra's back while I did all I could to calm him, Liam keeping the three others in eyes view in case they decided to run off, but they seemed more docile than the rest, curious even.

Liam relaxed his body and slowly turned back into his human self, injuries and all still present and then they seemed to fizzle away as he healed.

"What is going on?" one of the men asked.

"Cannibalism, if you will..." my lips trembling at the thought as the words forced their way out in a raspy whisper.

"Have you fed?" Liam asked.

"Fed on what? Everyone who was human here, isn't anymore or they've run south." One explained.

"How many turned?" Liam asked.

"I couldn't tell you, so many died from the bites, the ones who didn't turned just died from their injuries. We had a population of at least two hundred at Montgomery, mostly guards. Women and children were all airlifted out before the worst struck." he explained.

Ezra had calmed enough to return to his human form and the rest of us waded in the water as the flames surrounded us, they were jarringly loud. I didn't realize just how loud fire could be. It bent and snapped and exploded things that I didn't even consider possible, I'd never been in the middle of a fire though. Noah and Christian had lived this life, they'd endured this uncertainty with an endurance I could have never had as a human. It was a different pressure than what I was used to.

"Are you okay?" I asked Ezra.

"I need you to tie me up. I don't want to do that to any of you." He sighed as he splashed his face with the water from the river and a stream of red flowed down his bare chest.

Blood flowed freely from his mouth as he rinsed out chunks of flesh and splintered bone from between his teeth. His expression was blank, and his once cheeky grinned was hardened and a shadow of disgusted lurked behind the desire.

"Bro, that was nuts." Austin grasped his shoulder without hesitation.

"Don't touch me, I don't want to hurt you." Ezra pulled away, his eyes still red and dark.

He was in obvious pain; pain from the loss of Carrie or pain from what had just happened I wasn't sure, but he was so close to that unforgiving edge.

"Celinde?" Liam questioned my thoughts.

"She's on her own now." I sighed.

"What? You're going to just let her go out there on her own?" Austin growled.

"We've got three hostages and one incoherent Ezra. I'm going to bank on her being safer away from us." I argued.

"Christian would never…" Austin snapped.

"Christian would never put Celinde in harm's way." I stood over him and tried to reassure some the logic of it.

"He's right, Austin. She's got a better chance without us."
Ezra backed me even as his words were a stutter and he
fiddled with a chipped tooth.

"Fine, everything's falling apart anyway." He moved to
the other side of the bank through the sludge alone.

We all followed the new three members of our group;
they were careful not to overstep. They seemed
interested. They were obviously afraid of becoming
Ezra's next snack. A good way to be around a werewolf
that's gone cannibal. I knew what Ezra did was out of
necessity. I knew he did it to buy me time, but at his own
expense. I also knew he was so fucked up over the loss of
Christian and Carrie he might not care enough to resist
the rest of us. I pushed the thought out of my mind and
tried to focus on recruiting the new guys.

"Names?" I demanded.

"Cole, Rhett and I'm James." He pointed to each one of
them.

Cole was tall, lean with blonde hair. Rhett was slightly
older, blue steel for hair, the kind of guy who looked like
he never missed a day of work, the good neighbor. James
was the youngest, he had dark hair and a poorly grown
beard, the patchy type where a moustache was only
acceptable for movember.

"You all know each other?" I asked.

"Barely, we've served a few overnight watches together on the towers. Nothing big." Cole answered.

"You all from here?" I questioned.

"I'm from Kansas City, Coles from North Carolina and James is from Florida." Rhett answered.

"First thing you need to know about being a werewolf, don't ever feed on a human or another werewolf, killing one is different to feeding." I looked them all dead in the eyes.

"Humans?" Cole was puzzled.

"You start feeding and then you can't stop, that's how this shit happens." Austin threw up his arms and looked at Montgomery ablaze behind us.

"How do you know that?" Rhett asked.

"We've been werewolves a lot longer than you might think." Ezra snarled.

The others did their best to avoid eye contact with Ezra and kept their eyes ahead of them.

"Who was that back there who got killed?" Cole asked.

"Were you there?" Austin's ears pricked up at the question.

"Yeah." He nodded.

"Ezra's girl, and Jax's best friend." Liam answered.

I seemed to be running out of friends too quickly, they were all dropping like flies now.

The next step was a no-brainer – survive.

What that meant exactly, I had no idea. I was terrified. Not for myself, but for anyone out there who had survived the brunt of the attacks. The strong, the lucky, the now unlucky. It was an impossible future ahead of them. A life on the run, we would outlive them, outrun them and finitely – consume them.

Resisting the urge to feed was getting harder by the minute. Human food was becoming scarce and staving off the hunger wouldn't last long under these conditions. I was at risk of becoming the worst version of myself, we all were.

It was equally harder to encourage human-like behavior without human food. As days passed our newcomers became famished with hunger and so were the rest of us. I think the only thing that kept them at bay was the fear of being made the meal themselves and even as they fought through their own discomforts and transformations, they did it with grace and mostly silence to not irritate Ezra. They'd witnessed what wrath could ensue.

We came across a deserted gas station; everything in sight was abandoned, cars, RV's, strollers. Everything was empty, not a body in sight or breath to be heard.

"We'll take shelter in here tonight." I announced as rain pelted down on the old tin roof.

It was far from comfortable. The only food left behind were rotting boiled peanuts, chewing gum and the odd cockroach that lurked amongst the remains of what was once the crisps aisle— a smorgasbord of insects and rodents were the only other things on offer.

Ezra snatched at a large roach and regrettably choked it down even fighting against his gag reflex he swallowed it back.

"Bro…" Austin was squeamish, and he looked as though he might heave.

"Better *it*, than you." He grunted as he flung metal rails about searching for more sustenance.

"Valid point." Cole agreed and he began to help Ezra search.

"I'm glad she can't see how far I've fallen." Ezra sighed as he grasped a small mouse from the open fridge door and slumped to his feet taking his time with it.

His fangs grew as he dangled the mouse above his face. He tore at it as if he were trying to make it stretch that little bit further.

"Get some sleep, we should move on from here once daylight hits." I warned. Carrie sprung to mind as I watched over Ezra.

She'd hate this, she'd never have let this happen. Collectively with Carrie and Celinde we were a complete person and that's how we survived for so long. Carrie was the heart, Celinde held all the emotions, Mindy was the nurturer, Alexa was playful and free spirited, the rest of us were just the muscle— worthless muscle that lay dormant for years.

If we had any sense, we would have scrubbed the country clean of werewolves. At least that's what Lupe would have done; she didn't hesitate to fire up the Precinct once she saw what was happening to us. I just didn't have the strength she had. Her days moping in sorrow were a distant memory, that's not how I'd remember her, she was strong and what she endured took courage.

But who knew how many more wild celestial events could affect us.

Ezra barely slept a wink; he was easily stirred and would thrash around creating more noise than I'd like to have coming out of this place.

"You've got to tie me up, Jax!" Ezra demanded as he hurled a length of rope at me as he writhed in pain trying not to morph into his alternate self.

"Bro…" I huffed hesitantly.

"Jax! Do it. Tomorrow we'll find another way, but right now I need your help." Ezra pleaded as his eyes rolled back into his head as he fought off his alter ego.

Ezra never begged, he was always the cool, calm, collected, dreadlocked hipster I had met in Kamloops. He was the first one I trusted, the next best thing I had to Christian, it burned me to see him like this, to see him weak and broken. This wasn't him— he had fallen so far in such little time.

"It's going to be okay." I lied as I tied him up as best I could, but we both knew the ropes didn't stand a chance. They were old and brittle, some fraying began as he moved his arms, and I sucked in a deep breath.

"You've never been good at lying, Jax." he chuckled through a raspy cough and spluttered some blood into his palm.

I dropped to my knees and let out a sigh. I had no words of comfort for him, I had no idea what we were going to do. Do we just succumb to the anarchy around us, do we fight it, do we embrace it. My questions were many, yet I found myself speechless and still full of ponder with no solution.

"By all means keep the rest of us awake." Austin yawned.

"Sorry." I grunted.

"Not like you were really sleeping anyway." Ezra scowled.

"I was trying; pretty hard with that oaf snoring." he glared at Rhett fast asleep.

"Want me to deal with them?" Ezra's eyes darkened as his fingers began to shed their nails and reform with a thick claw.

"NO!" I growled as I stood over Ezra.

"You might not have to." Austin announced with alarm in his voice as he peered out of the covered window.

"There's others out there." he cowered back kicking Liam awake.

"Shhh." I whispered softly.

"Let them pass through, no noise." I ordered as I lay on the ground several feet away from Ezra trying to stay out of sight of the cracks in the window covers.

He was trying his hardest not to lash out, but it was useless. Ezra broke through the ropes and smashed through the glass windows and disappeared into the darkness. The only sign of him was the screams and sounds of his wrath that followed his loud thuds.

"Stay here." I ordered as I peered through the broken window with shards of glass still intact. The trees were dark, the night sky violent with a storm blocking the only light we had from the moon and a wind that whipped angrily.

The air grew quieter as I listened harder. Then the screams dulled. The pressure in my ears built as I heard limbs being torn from bodies and blood dripped to the ground and splattered over trees—I heard every trickle.

"We need to go after him." Austin whispered in my ear.

"What if he's too far gone now?" Liam questioned.

"He was barely keeping it together." Liam added.

"We can't just leave him." Austin grimaced.

"I'm going! stay here." I ordered as I slipped out of the window and bounded into the direction of the sound of butchery.

I approached slowly; Ezra wasn't himself; he was human now – but barely and I watched as he fed on the bodies that lay at his feet.

"I hear you Jax…" He hissed through his mouthfuls of death.

"Are you okay?" I asked reluctantly as I shifted through the mess of freshly broken trees and showed myself.

"I've never felt more alive." He smiled with red eyes and threw a bone in my direction.

"Come on, you've had your fun, it's time to go." I demanded.

"I'm not coming with you." Ezra stood up from the ground pushing away the mound of slaughtered bodies.

"Yes, you are. I need to look out for you." I sighed at my overwhelming position to care for the remainder of our group.

"If I come with you; you'll never sleep, you'll never eat and you'll be watching your back for the rest of your existence. Let me go, Jax…" Ezra sighed with a serious tone now.

"I can't." I relaxed my shoulders.

"You have to —Look after Liam and Austin for me." Ezra grasped my shoulder, blood, and hair not of his own coated his face. I could see it pained him to be this close to me.

The desire to kill anything that drew breath was deep in his veins now. His struggle was visible, more so than before. Every victim he took, the more the werewolf took of him.

"I can't do this without you." my eyes welled up.

"Yes, you can. You're the strongest man I know." he pressed.

"Ez, I can't just let you run wild and free." I growled.

"You don't have it in you to put down another friend either." His teeth barred in a mischievous smile—he knew me well.

He knew every loss was instant and never calculated, that made this the worst of all. When you know it's coming, but you're helpless to stop it...

"Go, before I kill you." I closed my eyes.

I felt the wind lash past my face as the weight of Ezra's body licked the wind in front of me one last time.

"Goodbye, friend." I wept as I stared at the stars through a small opening in the clouds. The moonlight hit my cheeks and my eyes opened yellow.

Hunter's Moon: Caged

V.J.Garland

Chapter Two

Celinde

I was lost deep in the woods now. Surrounded by nothing but my fear, sadness, and a surprising feeling of relief.

I wasn't alone, I knew that much. These woods were full of life, I did my best to stay away from anything that moved. My shoes were old and worn and barely offered enough cushioning to help me scale the rocks and fallen branches. I felt everything through the paper-thin soles and worn rubber.

It took me days till I found a small group of humans. I stayed a good distance away from them, so I wasn't noticeable. I felt safer in their company even at a distance. They were heavily armed and hunted along their route. They seemed to be collecting carcasses as they moved further to the east and using them as they went. There were so many times I wanted to sneak into their encampment as they slept and take just a morsel of food. They dried strips of jerky and ate well even if was a purely carnivorous diet.

I was underweight; I had been for years, but more so now. I was weak and had no access to food or water, I was just a bleak resemblance of what I once was, a shell.

I don't know where I was when it happened, but I blacked out for what felt like a good few days, and when I woke those four men were carrying me on a makeshift stretcher.

"Who are you?" I asked as I rubbed my head.

They all came to a stop and sat me down; one bearded man offered me water as he held me up to drink.

"We're just a bunch of survivors, we're heading to Manhattan. The island has been declared a safe zone." one answered.

They sat around me as I gathered myself, their backs to me and their guns loaded and ready.

"So edgy…" I exclaimed.

"These woods aren't safe." another replied.

"What's your name?" One asked.

"I'm Celinde." I answered.

"This is Mateo." He was tall with dark hair and features, not the kind of guy who said a lot, but he had this focus about him that made me not want to look at him.

"This is Getty." He was similar in looks to Mateo. They could easily pass for brothers if they weren't.

"This is Zeek." Zeek scared me, he had this wildness in his eyes, I didn't like it when he looked at me; he was lean and his height went on forever, with blue bloodshot eyes from lack of sleep and a weak beard for someone middle-aged, Carrie would say he had the crazy in him—And he did.

"I'm Zane." Zane was the bearded one and who I could only assume to be the leader of their group, he was better with people and had a warm nature about him.

They didn't talk amongst themselves much; they barely made any noise at all. They were cautious and so they should be.

"Where did you come from?" Zane whispered softly as he propped himself up beside me.

"North." I said with a shallow breath.

"Were you alone?" He asked.

"No." I sighed as my eyes welled with tears.

His eyes took me in as I sunk my face between my legs and gasped through my pain.

He was careful when comforting me, his hand hesitant but attentive and he warmed my back with his touch.

The others walked a perimeter around us as I thoughtlessly drank Zane's water rations and choked down dried oatmeal and painfully crisp jerky.

Zane was patching my shoes with duct tape as I washed my face with the last of his water.

"Thank you." I sighed as he examined my weathered feet.

"We'll get you some new shoes when we get to the others." He nodded as he pulled my shoes on for me.

"It's been a while." I agreed.

"These shoes look like they've been through more than a month of this life?" He was curious about me and building a backstory to boot.

"I was at the first outbreak." I wasn't going to lie, not entirely.

"And you survived? You must be tough." He patted my shoulder.

He didn't press me for more information, he didn't need to know more, not yet. That was too much for anyone, it was too much for me. I'd literally been a werewolf, even if only for a bleep of a lifetime.

Zeek's eyes burned as he watched me closely. He was sniffing me out like a hungry dog.

Zane decided we'd camp in this spot for the night. There was running water in a creek, and they were well prepared with personal water filter straws. I didn't feel so guilty about using all of the water once I saw them pull those out.

In a past life, I'd assume these guys were preppers, they had everything, dehydrated food, military-grade flints, even the odd MRE was passed around.

"Who are you guys?" I asked.

"We were marines, but when the government crumbled, we were just the last ones standing, we were stationed out at Virginia Beach when the worst of it hit." Mateo explained.

"That makes sense." I nodded.

"Which part?" Zeek asked.

"All the same haircuts." I replied politely.

"Giggle, giggle." He mocked my humor.

"I wasn't trying to offend…" I stuttered.

"Shut up, Zeek. She's been through enough." Mateo challenged him.

"She's another mouth to feed." he grumbled.

"Well technically, you eat more than her." Zane laughed as he challenged him in my favor.

Getty laughed loudly and splashed Zeek with some water.

"He got you there." Getty chuckled.

"Can she fire a gun? Can she kill and skin a deer?" He glared at me expecting I'd be some useless expenditure.

"Yes, I can." The others were surprised at my immediate response.

I wasn't the best, but I'd learned a lot from Carrie and the others in all my years at the Precinct.

"I can tell the difference between a good werewolf and a hungry werewolf. I know how to kill a werewolf. I might be more valuable than you might think, Zeek!" I growled.

"You can't kill a werewolf, not easily." Zeek snarled.

"Think again, I know how to kill them with so much as a hose." I was betraying my family now. I was selling my soul for MREs and filtered water.

"Tell me more." Zane demanded my focus.

"Silver." I was reluctant to spill the full details.

"We tried all the fairytale stuff; silver bullets don't work." He laughed.

"Wrong silver." I whispered.

Shut up Celinde! I was scolding myself inside. Jax and Ezra were still out there, Liam and Austin, the others who didn't join us. If this information fell into the right hands, I'd be sending them straight to the infernos of hell. I'd just lost my best friend and the love of my life. I knew I wasn't thinking straight, but I was in a position where I might need to use this knowledge to ensure my survival.

"What other kind is there?" Zeek probed.

"Liquid." I sighed. I had all intentions of saying nothing, but it just spilled out of me.

"Would give it time to hit the bloodstream," Zane thought aloud.

I wasn't about to correct him, if he wanted to assume I meant melted-down silver then he could stew on that for as long as it took him to figure out that it didn't work.

I laid down in the thin sleeping bag Zane had offered me. He kept close to me as if he knew I wasn't even safe amongst his comrades. They didn't communicate the way friends would —only by necessity.

My belly was full, but my sleep was horrendous. I had branches poking every limb and the sound of snoring was inescapable. Getty was the worst; it was this crazy deep inhale, and his exhale was a dry gurgle. He was a beacon in the darkness for an attack from humans or werewolves, even wildlife.

The trees shook in the wind, and I was awoken by the warmth of the sun. I hadn't felt the warmth of the sun on my cheeks like this in a long time. I got up before the others and walked down to the stream washed myself as best I could and took the time to urinate without being watched.

"You shouldn't be down here alone." It was Mateo.

"I needed some privacy." I used a suggestive facial expression.

"Hmm." he sighed as he turned around and relieved himself.

"Ugh, you couldn't have done that away from me." I grumbled.

"This is the bathroom." he laughed.

I could smell his urine; it was strong, and I knew immediately he was dehydrated.

"That stinks." I coughed from a distance.

"Does yours smell like roses?" he laughed as he zipped up his old pants.

I pushed past him and examined his urine which still lingered in the water with a different viscosity.

"When did you last drink any water?" I asked.

"Maybe once a day, not often." he mumbled.

"You're dehydrated, badly. Go and drink some water." I ordered.

"What are you, a doctor?" he scoffed.

"No, Mateo. I'm just a paramedic, but I know enough to know your urine shouldn't be brown." I hissed back.

"Go and drink some water." Zane ordered from afar. He was standing a few feet away from us watching our exchange.

"I'm fine." Mateo argued.

"Not worth risking it." Zane replied.

Mateo walked off and took the water filter straw and sat by the stream and cupped handfuls of water and drank through the pipe while Getty filled a collapsible bucket to be filtered.

"Medic?" Zane looked at me.

"Past life…" I muttered as I turned away.

"How many lives have you had?" he probed.

"More than I deserve." I replied.

"You're quite the mystery woman." He smiled.

"How so?" I entertained his assumptions.

"Well, you were a medic, you were there at the first outbreak, you know how to kill werewolves that have seemingly only been around for a month, give or take. But your shoes tell me you've been running for years. What are you running from?" He questioned.

"I've been running so long I don't even remember, myself." I sighed.

"I don't believe you." he grumbled.

"I don't expect you to." I replied.

"You're not going to tell me everything are you?" He asked.

"No." I answered.

"Who did you lose to this?" he pressed.

"Everyone…" I surrendered.

"That can't be true, I've never seen a female turn." His expression twisted.

I got up and began walking, I didn't care if I stayed with them or not, I just needed to keep moving.

"Time to move!" I heard Zane order the others as he raced behind me.

"Look, you can be as cryptic as you like with me, but there are others who won't let you get away with being so dismissive." he warned me as his eyes trailed to Zeek.

"I'm not going with you." I scowled.

"Sorry, but you are! We need medics." He grabbed my arms and tied my wrists together.

"Let me go!" I fought.

"I didn't want to do this Celinde, but if you won't come willingly, I have no choice." Zane sighed.

"What are you going to do with me?" I screamed.

"Shut her up!" Getty began stuffing dirty fabric in my mouth while Zeek taped it around my face, the tape pulling at my hair as it wrapped all the way around my head.

"Not so rough!" Zane growled.

"Too much talking Zane, you could have had her back without any fuss if you stopped trying to make friends." Zeek laughed as he stroked my cheek.

I was in bad company and suddenly grateful I hadn't completely exposed my situation.

I wasn't about to make this easy for them, so I sat myself down and held my weight as best I could. It was hopeless, Zane was a marine, he was built fit and strong and stood almost as tall as Jax and Christian, easily over 6"1 but he was broad and had a natural power to him.

He picked me up with ease and swung me over his shoulder and continued walking. We stopped for breaks only twice, he never let the others carry me. I was afraid for my safety; I didn't know what was waiting for me. An encampment of horny marines and I was the flavor of the month. I didn't know the kind of people whose hands I had fallen into—the possibilities terrified me.

"Almost there." Zane whispered to me as I struggled with my discomfort.

I couldn't reply, my eyes did the talking for me, they were dull and swollen—like my heart.

V.J.Garland

Chapter Three

Zane

She was skeletal and giving me joint pain in my shoulder from her bony frame digging into me. I knew she'd never walk if I asked her. Zeek wasn't to be trusted. He would just as soon pick her up and disappear with her. The others could care less if she came or not.

"Can you stay still?" I grumbled as we climbed a hill.

She kicked and swung her body in protest as best she could. I gently dropped her to the ground. She landed in a heap covered in dirt.

"I can give you to Zeek if you like?" I tore down her duct tape from her lips and caused them to bleed as I whispered the threat in her ear.

"NO!" She knew he wasn't all there and quickly submitted with a nod.

"I'll walk!" she hissed.

The others watched on as I allowed her to travel beside me on her own two legs. She was wobbly and badly needed a decent meal. She looked as though she had been living on slim rations for years.

"Is that wise?" Getty asked.

"I'll stay put." she assured me as she tugged at my sleeve somewhat afraid, like a little kid who was being punished.

I held her gaze and a trust formed between us. She knew I was the least likely to hurt her. Zeek would just as soon use and abuse her and throw her to any raiders or werewolves we stumbled across.

We weren't far from the base outside of Charlotte, but the sounds that loomed around us got closer and warned us to stay back. Getty and Zeek climbed a hill and used their scopes to check out the area below. What they saw was bad, the biggest pack of werewolves we'd come across yet.

"We'll be lucky if they don't catch us." Getty whispered.

"What are they doing down there?" Celinde asked.

"Plotting." Zeek scowled.

A lot were in their human forms, others around them were beasts, watching the perimeter.

"We need to get out of here." Mateo said frantically.

"Calm down! we don't want to draw any attention." I tried to stay composed.

We gathered our belongings and began to trek south. We'd have to go around the long way if we wanted to make it to Manhattan eventually and avoid that encampment.

"We need to hunt; we don't have enough food." Getty whispered as he shuffled through an empty zip-lock bag that once housed the jerky.

"Bows, no firearms. The sound will travel to them." Zeek ordered.

"Are you okay?" I poked Celinde.

She wasn't responding, she was in a daze and just kept walking without being directed. Her presence was almost lifeless, she could almost go unnoticed, she was so light-footed and quiet.

"She's weird." Zeek joked.

"No, she's afraid." I muttered.

I knew what fear looked like, it closed you off from the world and locked you in a box you couldn't escape. You couldn't hear or feel anything anyone was doing around you. It made you suffer within yourself. Your body became a cage of torture that punished you with your own thoughts.

I walked closely behind her as she stumbled across the land in her badly worn shoes. I knew those shoes had a story, a story I had to know. Celinde knew more than she was letting on, but she was never going to tell me everything.

"There's a house." Getty pointed out.

"Approach slowly." I motioned forward with my hands.

Zeek and Mateo descended the hill first and checked out the house.

It was clear and they signaled for us to come down a few moments later.

"I'd feel safer outside." Celinde objected as we reached the front door.

"You guys go in; I'll stay with her." I nodded as they all rummaged through the remains of the homestead.

"You should get some rest." Celinde looked at me and sighed.

"So should you." I retorted.

Getty was going through the cupboards in the kitchen and Mateo had found a doorway to a hidden basement, he was down there scouring the shelves.

"How big is it down there?" I asked through the window.

"Pretty big; lots of canned food." Mateo answered.

"Pull out some food, we'll sleep here tonight." I ordered.

"What if whoever lives here comes back?" Celinde argued.

"Whoever lived here is dead." Zeek flung the door open and pointed at the barely fried blood splatter on the inside of the door.

"Comforting." she rolled her eyes at him.

She pulled herself up from the porch and headed inside to lie on the sofa in the middle of the room.

Zeek lit a fire on the wood-burning stove while Mateo cleared the messy dining table. Getty patrolled outside and I watched the back entrance while we let Celinde rest.

Her sleep was disrupted with vivid dreams, she never seemed truly at rest. She had been through trauma, and it showed in every state of mind.

"Should we wake her?" Getty observed her body jolting sporadically.

"No, she's just dreaming." I sighed.

"You're sure it's not a seizure?" Mateo asked.

"It's not." I assured him as I scooped myself a bowl of canned braised beef and vegetables.

I sat on the ground in front of her letting the others use the only three chairs in the house.

"We'll leave in the morning." Getty announced.

He was alert and concerned about our surroundings. The convening of such a large pack was definitely something to be worried about.

"Zane…" Celinde whispered as her hand touched my beard.

"You must be hungry." I turned to face her. Her eyes were heavy, and that small sleep did nothing for the dark bags under her dull blue eyes.

"Famished." she said as she rubbed her face.

I got up from the ground and fetched her a bowl of food as she sat up and rubbed her sore bare feet.

"It's not great." I chuckled as I handed her the bowl.

"I'll take anything right about now." She smiled with only the good side of her lips. "Zane, I'm sorry I gave you a hard time before." she added.

I sat on the couch beside her, and I rubbed her bony back as she ate away slowly at the mush in the bowl.

"Cozy over there…" Getty made insinuations.

"Just be grateful she chose the couch and not one of the three single beds." I snapped.

"Fair game." Mateo smiled and leaped for the bedroom.

The others inhaled their food faster and dashed for the other rooms determined to cheat me out of a decent night's sleep.

"I'll take watch if you want the couch?" Celinde stood up and took my empty bowl from the coffee table as if cleaning up would make a difference.

"Just for a few hours, wake me up if you need me." I grasped her wrist and made myself clear in a firm tone.

"I'm not going to run off." she assured me.

"Stay inside, watch from the windows." I ordered.

"Zane, I've done this before…" she reminded me as she trotted towards the kitchen.

I watched over her from the couch until my eyes became heavy; it didn't take long. Suddenly I was away in another place and time. I was at my family ranch; my dad was barbecuing. I was throwing my sister Jessie's kids into the pool, and my mom was chopping fresh salads while my brother-in-law mowed their lawn with a beer in hand. It's what we did when I wasn't away on tour with the military. The old family cat was rolling on the sun-kissed concrete bounding after butterflies over the small bushes and trotting through the long grass. Jessie's dog would drink the koi pond water and curiously gawk at the fish when they came up for air equally just as curious about the dog.

Sleep was so sought after, yet I couldn't obtain it for longer than an hour.

Celinde was sat on the windowsill staring out into the darkness, her eyes glimmered into the moonlight drenched with silent tears that soaked her sunken cheeks.

I got up from the couch and moved closer to her and sat within her reach if she wanted a hug.

"If you wanna talk about it, I'm told I'm a good listener." I brushed her arm reluctantly.

"To be honest with you, I don't even know where to begin." she wiped her cheeks.

"What hurts the most?" I asked.

"A couple days before you guys found me my boyfriend and my best friend were killed. Then I got separated from the rest of our group." she explained.

"I'm so sorry." I held her hand gently.

"He became a werewolf. A good one, he never hurt anyone. Do you believe there are good ones?" She asked as she locked my eyes in hers.

"I believe everyone has a choice to be the best or worst version of themselves." I stuttered.

In truth I didn't believe my own words, I understood the reality that what she went through would have been very real and difficult but now I knew she had some sort of inner knowledge of how they worked. She had to know their weakness.

"Thank you." she squeezed my hand.

"What did I do? I smiled.

"There's just a comfort in your optimism." she turned back to the window.

"We should pack some food and be ready to go when the sun comes up." I urged as I walked off to the basement.

"Are we far away from your other people?" She asked as she followed behind me.

"We're just a bunch of small groups, we all meet at an old hospital in Philadelphia," he explained.

"We aren't too far away?" She questioned.

"Another day or so." I answered.

"Great…" she muttered.

"You can do this." I tossed her cans of beans as she packed them into a bag.

It was clear the exhaustion she felt ran deep, her malnutrition a big factor in it all. If she wasn't so valuable, I'd be tempted to leave her behind, but she wasn't dead weight anymore, she was knowledge, and I felt a sense of pity for her.

"Sun's coming up, wake the others." She said as she packed the rest of the rice into a sack.

I climbed the stairs where Mateo was yawning, he was on the lookout for more food.

Celinde hurled a bag at him as she panted her way up and I went to wake Getty and Zeek.

"Let's go." I kicked Zeek gently.

"It's barely light out." he groaned.

"We need every second of daylight we can get, they're stronger at night." I growled back.

Getty was up and pulling his boots on, Zeek was not as forthcoming, but he rolled out slowly and forced himself up.

"Keep low." Celinde said as she listened to the low growls in the forest of werewolves in the distance.

She handed Zeek the heavier bags and kept close behind me as we tracked our way further north.

The sun burned hot against the cool breeze as we hiked further into the backcountry of the Appalachian Mountains through Pennsylvania. The terrain was rugged and unforgiving and there was a loom in the woods that stalked our movements. Werewolf or human, or maybe something else? We couldn't be sure.

We arrived back at our base as the sun began to set. Getty, Mateo, and Zeek took the food supplies and kills to the kitchen inside the old hospital we had boarded up into a shelter. There weren't many survivors here; six others, mostly other marines who had escaped from Virginia with us and whoever else rolled in from neighboring groups. As long as they weren't werewolves, they were *mostly* welcome if they followed our rules.

"Come with me." I said to Celinde as I led her down a long-darkened hallway.

"Where are you taking me?" She hesitated.

"Somewhere you can rest." I replied.

I knew I needed her to trust me before I could extract information from her.

We entered what used to be an operating room, it was large and painfully white with a pile of sterile mattresses and pillows piled into two corners.

"It's not much, but it'll be comfier than anything you've had in a while." I nodded.

"Thank you, Zane." she whispered as she clutched a pillow close to her and buried her face in it.

"Make yourself at home. I'll see what's for dinner and bring some up." I dumped my pack on another mattress and raced down the stairs to the kitchen.

"Hey boys!" I announced as I met with our designated cook, Lincoln.

"My man!" Lincoln pulled me into a man hug and pounded his fist on my back.

"Still kicking." He added.

"I was graced with another day." I laughed.

"He was also graced with a woman." Mateo laughed as he snuck into the kitchen.

"I hope you caught a few extras for the rest of us." Lincoln teased.

"It's not like that, she knows something. I need to earn her trust and find out what it is." I explained.

"Something like what?" Lincoln asked.

"She knows about werewolves, I think she knows the origin and maybe how we can defeat them, at least control them. She seems to have some empathy towards them, her boyfriend was one." I explained.

"Well butter her up and bring her some of this." He handed me a plate with two hotdogs covered in cheese, chili, and a side of fries.

"Where did you get that?" Mateo's mouth watered.

"Miles and Eleazar found a deli basically untouched a few streets over, the generators were just about to run out." he smiled.

"What else was in there?" I asked.

"Everything, cigarettes, ice cream, frozen food, cheese, some ammo." He tossed me a box of cigarettes.

"I don't smoke." I hurled the box at Mateo.

"Neither do I, but now I do." he smiled as he raced out to the others.

"Let's try and ration, who knows if we'll get that lucky again." I sniffed at the hotdogs.

"And a plate for you." He handed me a plate of food for myself.

"Get out of my kitchen and feed that woman." Lincoln laughed.

I walked back up the stairs and down the hallway to where I had left Celinde, she was curled up on a bed with a scratchy hospital blanket wrapped around her.

"You awake?" I whispered.

"Yeah." she said softly.

"Here's your dinner, ma'am." I smiled as I leaned down to pass her the plate and I sat in front of her on the ground and began eating my food.

"Woah, it's been so long since I've had one of these." her eyes lit up.

"The boys got lucky on a surveillance run." I smiled.

"Compliments to the chef of frozen goods!" she smiled through a mouthful.

"Is this your room?" she asked as she looked around at the other bed that I had often slept in.

"Yeah, I prefer to be away from the others." I sighed.

"Prefer your own company, I respect that." she nodded through another mouthful.

"If I slept in the same room as Zeek every night I might choke him out." I confessed.

"He gives me the creeps." She admitted.

"Rightfully so, he's not to be trusted." She knew I was serious by the tone of my voice.

"Noted." she agreed.

"You tired?" I asked.

"A little, slightly wired though." she sighed.

"That's fair, you're in a new place." I nodded.

"Don't suppose there's any showers that work?" She asked.

"Right through that door." I point to the other side of the room.

"Any feminine products by any chance?" she asked shyly.

"What kind?" I asked.

"The monthly kind." she replied.

"Oh... let me check." I got up and wrestled through boxes of compound bandages and tubes.

Celinde stood up carefully trying to cover herself, but she had bled through her clothes and there was a stain in the bedding she had rested in. She pulled at the sheet and brought it with her to the shower.

"We'll just burn it." I stopped her as I grasped the sheet.

"No, for what dignity I have left, I need to do this." She pulled it into her.

"Suit yourself, there's plenty where that came from." I pointed to a linen cupboard.

She beelined for the shower and filled the bathroom with steam as I hunted around for sanitary pads and clothing for her.

I raced down the stairs to the kitchen and interrogated Lincoln.

"Linc, we got any girl stuff around?" I asked.

"Like what?" He asked.

"Clothes, menstrual stuff?" I explained.

"Oh, the poor love. On the maternity ward, I think Getty said there was a bunch of that stuff." He walked with me to the stairwell.

"I'll come with you." He followed behind me somewhat suspiciously.

"Thanks, I don't know what I'm looking for." I laughed as I brushed off the feeling.

"You never had a girlfriend before?" He joked.

"Yeah, but I'm never home long enough to be here for that." I laughed.

"Over there." he pointed to a hallway cupboard with sanitary pads of all different shapes and sizes, tampons, and heat packs.

"One of everything and I'll fill up a hot water bottle for her." Lincoln ordered as he raced down the stairs to fill the hot water bottle.

The cupboard had towels, gowns, scrubs, underwear, and crop tops. I guessed the sizes and took a bunch downstairs to her; she was still in the shower.

"You, okay?" I poked my head in with my eyes closed.

"Yeah." she seemed to be weeping.

"I found some towels and clothes." I placed them on the chair beside the shower curtain.

"Thanks." she shouted through the water.

"There's every kind of sanitary pad you could dream of as well, I'll leave them on the bench." I said as I placed them down.

She was silent as she sat in the heat. The steam built on the mirror in heavy droplets and cascaded into the sink.

"Okay, I'm going to bed." I left the room and undressed down to my underwear and made my bed.

Celinde exited the bathroom in a hospital gown looking for somewhere to hang her wet clothes she had washed in the shower.

"Goodnight." she whispered looking me up and down.

"Goodnight." I yawned.

I climbed into my small bed and closed my eyes tightly trying to transport myself to another time, another memory, a time when things weren't so hard.

V.J.Garland

CHAPTER FOUR

EVAN

The fires from the Precinct took weeks to subside. Winter was turning to spring and the snow melted in a hurry against the heat.

Trekking south on foot was made easier as a werewolf, but as a werewolf, I felt the constant pain from when my arm had been hacked off. Although back intact I felt the plunge of the axe like it was yesterday. The healing was arguably worse, I felt the stings, pulls, and pinches like I was human again. It would take weeks, maybe even months to feel normal again, still enormously faster than a human. I was lucky to have a second chance to be whole at all.

I was alone in the world for the first time since I was born. My father had controlled not only the werewolf portion of my life but my entire existence. He had used me, abused me, and treated me like a tool in his efforts to broker ownership over different werewolf societies.

He was a lazy contributor. Narcissistic, arrogant, pessimistic, everything I had grown to despise in a person and werewolf. He had tried to instil a victim mentality in me. I was blind and lonely in a world that didn't accept me, and I stupidly ate up everything he served me out of desperation to find a place of comfort and belonging, because I simply didn't know any better.

It felt like a breath of fresh air to be free in the world. Jax likely thought I would be dead if he wasn't dead himself. I could still smell the scent of burning flesh, and singed hairs like it was glued to the inside of my nostrils. I could hear Lupina's screams as if she were right next to me, her voice was a constant ringing in my ears. The look on Noah and Jax's faces as they allowed her to decimate everything Jax had built, I don't know if they were both frozen in shock or just didn't want to hurt her any further, but they let her rage obliterate everything we had called home.

Lupina was different from Carrie, Mindy, Celinde, and all the others. They lived similar lives, but it was the company and aid of one another that set them aside. Lupina oozed loneliness, pain, and disgust for our kind.

Her hate for what we were could be felt in her eyes, she emitted a low and decrepit aura, and it was everywhere like a disease.

You could say she woke me up with her innocently kind face, but something was missing from her, one could argue it was her soul, but it wasn't, it was the love she had had stolen from her, she didn't have any left in her. I'd never seen someone without any love to give until I saw Lupina. I didn't even know it was a thing until she was there, and it smacked me in the face; she embodied all the hard years she had endured. She wore it like an amour and rode into battle with it and successfully destroyed the one thing that held significance to her—a home that wasn't a home, a prison.

I felt good being my own person, to think for myself, not being caged in by another person's orders.

I had kept myself a mile or so south of Kamloops. Close enough to food and supplies but far enough from humans if they saw me.

A white truck I was well acquainted with sped through the broken roads. It was Lucy and Alexa. I could hear Lucy yelling at Alexa from the road where I stood back in the tree line, and I followed them as they entered Kamloops.

Lucy was desperate to get home to McBride, but Alexa refused, trying to convince her everything and everyone was gone.

"I'll go alone, stay here!" Lucy pulled Alexa out of the truck, grinding it to a sudden halt.

"No!" She pushed her to the ground.

"You will die out there, get it through your head!" Alexa was pulling at her, her eyes teary.

"ALEXA!" Mindy screamed as she raced out of a motel.

"Mama!" Alexa pulled the keys from the ignition and ran to Mindy.

"BITCH!" Lucy leapt from the car slamming the door.

"Girls, what are you fighting over?" Mindy asked.

"She wants to go north." Alexa explained.

"I thought I'd never see you again." Mindy grabbed Alexa's face.

"Yeah, well there wasn't anywhere to go. It's a lot more hostile out there now. They're everywhere, there's nowhere to go, we've been driving around in circles." Alexa sighed.

I contemplated running down there and offering assistance to make up for my evil past, but I had tried to assault Alexa, my presence wouldn't be welcomed.

But in the same breath, I needed to feel human more than anything now. So, on a whim, I walked down the hill into the street and raised my arms in peace as I approached cautiously.

"Evan..." Mindy was a fearsome woman and an equally fierce mother. Her expression was guarded and striking, I feared her more than any werewolf in this moment.

She walked towards me without hesitation and punched me in the face, it barely rattled me, but I gave her the satisfaction and allowed myself to drop somewhat.

"I'm sorry!" I pleaded.

"You're sorry?" Alexa snarled.

"Yes, I wasn't thinking, I was being controlled." I sighed with my hands raised in the air again.

"Do you believe him?" Lucy asked.

"No, but he's alone and he's more trustworthy than anything else out there." Mindy sighed.

"Trustworthy?" Alexa screamed.

"He tried to rape me!" She yelled.

"I wasn't! I was trying to scare Tristan. I'd never rape you... I'm sorry I scared you." I sighed.

The height of my evil was the day I laid hands on Alexa. She was barely an adult. In my life, I'd mauled my way through small towns, and trailer parks, but I'd never felt more dominant than the day I took Alexa beneath me and touched her to threaten Tristan and I was so ashamed of myself.

"You can do whatever you want to me, Lex. I deserve it." I hung my head in shame.

She raced to the back of the truck and retrieved the old broken, rusting snow chains that were used to shield the tires.

"Prove it! On your knees..." she ordered as she flexed the chains.

I inhaled a deep breath, and my body shook in fear as I braced myself for the punishment she would lay on me.

"I'm going to make you feel as small as you made me feel." Her breathing was heavy as she fought back tears, and her words caught a little in her throat.

"Alexa, NO!" Mindy screamed.

"Leave her, she needs this." Lucy held Mindy back restraining her with her arms and turned her away so she wasn't watching what would unfold.

Mindy held onto Lucy's frame and buried her face into her shoulder as her hands held her ears as they tried to block out any sound. Alexa whipped the chains against the asphalt as a warning to me and Mindy's body jolted, and Lucy covered Mindy's her hands with her own as tears raced down her cheeks.

Alexa raised the chains and walked around to my back, and I sucked in one big deep breath. She rained the metal down on the back of my ribs. Every lashing cast blood into the road and every strike chipped or shattered a bone. My advanced healing struggled to keep up as I fell to the dirt road, my back torn and exposed and I felt the odd sheath of flesh flutter and then pull back and it took every ounce of strength not to turn, to use my beast as a shield.

"ENOUGH!" Lucy screamed.

Alexa ignored her pleas and moved around my body as I shook in shock laying on the floor.

She struck one last time, slamming the chains with all her might across my chest. I felt my ribs break and my chest deflate. I gasped for air, but I was before death now and the two sides of me raced to claim their right to my life.

Mindy rushed to my aid and collapsed over my body protecting me from further punishment. As mad as she was with me, she was always a caring soul, and she extended her nurturing nature upon me one last time.

Alexa was covered in my blood, her face now red. Lucy was cradling her face on the ground crying on her knees. My eyes were heavy, my body collapsed as I coughed blood, and my body played a vicious game of tug of war with itself between healing and giving up before I suddenly saw black.

I woke up in a room with nothing more than a bed and lamp. There were two doors and a clean set of clothes on the nightstand. I was healing, and while I wouldn't wear these scars forever, I would feel the mental and emotional damage for a lifetime and the next.

A knock at the door woke me a little more and then it opened, it was Alexa.

"Feel better?" she asked with bulging red eyes, she had been crying, but her face was mostly clean now.

"I'll be fine. do you feel better?" I sighed.

She sat on the bed beside me without flinching and I knew we had some found peace between us.

"I feel ashamed." she rubbed at the now crusty blood on her arms.

"I've felt that too." I sighed.

"I'm not ready to be your friend Evan, but we need you more than I need to hate you." she whimpered.

I moved my hand closer to her and she hesitantly grasped it as she took in a breath and squeezed softly.

"I respect you." I whispered.

"Don't ever disrespect me like that again." she choked back tears.

"I was a different person then." I admitted.

"You should go shower." she let go of me.

"I need a bit more time." I said as I shuffled and felt some broken bones grinding against each other.

"Knock, knock!" It was Mindy.

"Just making sure you two aren't going to keep trying to kill each other." she smiled awkwardly with a plate of sandwiches.

"This is big of you Mindy." I smiled curiously.

"People change, and right now there aren't many left in the world. What I know about you, Evan is that you were heavily influenced by your father. I know your father took your brother from you, I know you are capable of good things and while our world is broken and crippled, you can be a part of what makes your kind shine a little brighter. Jax and Arthur would have given you another chance, so will I." she brushed my hair off my face.

"Where is Arthur?" I asked.

"Hunting." she answered.

"He won't like seeing me." I sighed.

"Well, he's the only other werewolf here and there are hundreds of new and hungry werewolves heading north every day. We could use your help and he knows it." She explained.

"It's true, we didn't even make it to BC, and we could see the fires and hear them in the woods. That's why we turned around, we were running on fumes when we got here." Alexa agreed.

"Once I'm back on my feet I'll do what I can to help, I'll do whatever I can to earn your friendship." I sighed.

"We would appreciate that." Mindy smiled.

"I'm going to try and shower." I pushed through the blankets.

"Ugh, sorry. No running water, there's some buckets of water and a loofah." Mindy apologized.

"That's okay, I'll wait till I'm a little more healed in that case." I sunk my head.

"I'll help you." Alexa offered.

"It's the least I can do…" she added.

"You don't have to do that; I don't want to make you uncomfortable." I resisted.

"You're covered in blood and dirt because of me." She sighed.

"Look you two can go back and forth with that for days or I can help you into the shower and get to making dinner while she washes off that nastiness." Mindy interrupted.

"Mother knows best." I smiled as I tried to get out of bed.

Mindy was small but plump and did her best to hold my weight as I hobbled into the shower and onto a plastic chair. Alexa was foaming up a loofah with some water and the cheap hotel-brand body wash.

"Okay, you ready?" Alexa asked as Mindy left the room.

"Ready as I can be." I exhaled hard as I removed the last of my clothing, covering my manhood with the hand towel.

She seemed to take further pleasure in dumping the coldest bucket of water over my body.

"Arghh! That's ice." I shivered.

"Harden up, Evan." she joked.

I rubbed my face with a face towel as she scrubbed over my back softly.

"What are these?" She asked curiously as her fingers traced impalement wounds between my ribs.

I knew exactly what she meant...

"Evan? I know you don't scar unless another werewolf strikes you, but these are weird even for you." She exasperated.

"When I had just turned it's what Graham...dad, did to punish me if I disobeyed him." I began.

"What did he do?" She gasped.

"He would stab me with his claws and sink his fingers into me and scrape against my organs, if I was really bad, he'd use broken branches and make me fish out the splinters myself." tears filled my eyes, and I quickly wiped them away.

"I'm so sorry he was cruel to you." she sniffed.

"That's been my life, even long before the werewolf stuff, he was just a horrible person from every angle." I confessed.

"I didn't realize." She continued to scrub my body.

"It's fine, I'm good now." I nodded.

"We won't treat you like that—anymore." she gently lathered my hair with shampoo. Her touch changed dramatically. She was tender now, before she was purposely rough, trying to inflict one more dose of pain upon me.

Perhaps she saw the same traits in me as she did Tristan. Tristan was a good kid, but I heard about his wild and not-so-wonderful father. The werewolf who never was—Wesley.

"I'm sorry about Tristan." I sighed.

"I never wanted to hurt him, he was just such a likable orphan, it was easy to be jealous of him." I admitted.

"Tristan had a lot of demons; he didn't deserve this life, but I'm glad he was around. He brought me peace and distracted me. He helped me be a teenager when nobody else could. I hope I brought him a sense of peace after he lost his family." she sighed.

Their gravity towards one another made sense, they were close in age and with all the responsibilities Mindy and Arthur took on, Tristan took it upon himself to keep her safe when they were too busy to raise her. Tristan and Austin collectively taught her how to survive, and how to be bold, and gave her courage and the sense to survive like us.

"How old are you?" she asked.

"You don't know how old I am?" I laughed.

"No, it gets a little skewed with your kind." She raised a brow at me.

"twenty-five." I replied.

"Frozen at twenty-five you mean?" she asked.

"Well yeah but everything kind of just stops, I feel like I still think as if I'm a twenty-five-year-old. I don't feel my age, I couldn't even explain how old my body feels." I rubbed my ribs as I felt a bone snap into place.

"Is it painful for everyone?" she asked.

"Some worse than others, for me, I guess I got used to it, I wear it a little better, maybe. Rugged is just my look." I combed my fingers through my messy long hair.

"Rugged?" she laughed.

"What?" I asked.

"I would hardly describe you as rugged, maybe hipster with a dash of drug addiction." She poured clean water over me to remove the suds.

"I'll do my best to polish my appearance then." I grunted.

"No offense, none of us live a glamorous lifestyle." She sighed.

"Would you want glamour?" I questioned.

"We always want what we can't have." She replied.

"Who said you can't have it?" I asked.

"The world isn't what it was a year ago. Any hope of a normal life is gone." She muttered.

"Make your own normal, find new things to want." I said as I washed the lather from my hair.

She smiled a little crookedly and dried her hands before leaving the room so I could dry myself off.

I sat on the bed and ate the sandwiches Mindy had brought down for me. Alexa had gone to help her and Lucy.

I dressed in the clothes laid out for me and stripped the bed of the dirty sheets stained with my blood.

"I was about to do that." Alexa appeared with clean linens.

"You know you don't need to feel bad. You don't have to help me." I sighed.

"I don't feel bad, but we have to co-exist. Kindness is a good start." She said.

I wasn't used to kindness; Mindy was the kindest person I'd ever met. She was the first person I met at the Precinct, and she handed me a basket full of food and a hot meal with no questions asked. And I went and threw her hospitality in her face when I began doing my father's dirty work and trying to snatch it from under Jax.

"Pull the elastic over the corners." She ordered.

"Huh?" I was puzzled.

"You've never made a bed before, have you?" She asked.

"No, I wasn't born in a time when we had fitted bedding." I was slightly embarrassed.

"Okay, watch me." She shook out the fitted sheet pulled the elastic corners over each corner of the bed and laid on a flat sheet.

"Now you tuck the end under the mattress and fold the end up into the side of the bed and then fold the side flaps down. It looks tidier that way." She was so much like Mindy in that moment, nurturing and domestic.

"Wow, that does look nice." I smiled.

"Now you just put this on." She tossed me a comforter.

"Oh, and don't forget the pillowcases. You can manage those right?" She placed them on the bed.

"I'm sure I'll figure it out." I picked on up to examine it.

"Mama is going to bring you some pot roast soon." She said as she walked towards the door.

"Lex!" I called after her.

"Yeah?" she asked.

"Do you know if Lucy will go looking for Jax?" I asked.

"She was pretty worried about getting up to her parent's place in McBride. She hasn't talked about Jax and what happened, it still shakes her up." She explained.

"Okay." I replied.

"Why?" she asked leaning into the doorframe, her eyebrow peaked upward with its own curiosity.

"Thought I might try my luck at forgiveness." I sighed.

"If I know Jax and if Jax knew what I know now, you already have it." She smiled and turned out of the door.

I laid in bed for a while till I heard footsteps marching down the hallway and the smell of good home cooking wafted through my door first.

"Evan?" Mindy knocked at the door.

"Come in." Mindy came in with Arthur behind her.

"Arthur…" I lowered my head in shame.

"Never thought I'd see you again." Arthur scowled.

I could hear Lucy and Alexa's breathing as they stood back further down the hallway.

"I heard Alexa gave you quite a beating. Looks like she did a good job of it." He was observing the pile of blood-soaked linens in the corner and the open wounds still healing on my back.

"You would have been proud." I succumbed to him.

"Violence isn't something I normally stand for Evan, but in your case…" he lunged forward with his fists and ploughed a hit hard into my face breaking my nose.

"Damn it, Arthur!" Mindy placed down the food and rushed for a towel.

"OUCH!" I yelled.

Arthur straightened himself up and pulled away as he flexed his fist as if the hit hurt him more than it hurt me.

"I couldn't let her have all the glory. You can stay, but I'm watching you." he glowered.

"Dad I just changed those sheets." Alexa growled as he passed her in the doorway.

"Go to your room you two." Mindy ordered Alexa and Lucy away like they were little kids.

"He'll come around." she whispered as she placed the plate of food in my hands.

"Why have you?" I queried.

"Because I see you, Evan. I always knew you weren't the man your father forced you to be, you had your moments but you're capable of good things too." She smiled.

"Why were you so hard on Tristan then?" I asked.

"Tristan was never able to control his hunger, not completely… I guess every time he and Alexa ran off hunting, I was worried she'd be the body he brought back. He deserved better than I gave him. For that I regret how I treated him." she lowered her voice sadly.

"And you think I can do any better?" I asked.

"I know you can because if you don't, she'll hack your other arm off." Mindy laughed.

"I don't think I like the sound of that. Your daughter is a maniac." I laughed.

"Raised by werewolves." Mindy winked.

We're all on this floor, the kitchen is down the hall. Wash your dishes when you're done." she added as she left the room leaving me to eat in silence.

This was the first good meal I'd had in years. Potatoes that were cooked all the way through, salty and buttery with a crispy edge, roasted beef with a thick dark gravy, the perfect balance of pepper, and a wholesome cauliflower helping with a rich cheese sauce. I knew from what I was eating that Mindy was in a rush to use up produce. With the town emptied and threats from every angle, she'd spare no time or resource. Mindy was all about enriching our lives through food, offering us something more appetizing than warm veins and jerky muscles in the rigor mortis phase.

The meal was over too soon, but refuelling my body seemed to help speed up the last of my healing.

I paced the hall down to the kitchen and washed my dishes as Lucy sat peeling apples that were going brown.

"Those don't look so good." I said.

"Mindy said they'll be fine for an apple pie." Lucy replied.

"I won't argue then." I smiled.

"Do you think he's okay?" She fumbled through the apple peels.

"If anyone is okay, it's Jax." I nodded as I knew exactly who she was talking about.

"I shouldn't have left him." she sighed.

"I'm guessing you didn't have much of a choice with everyone going completely batshit crazy that night." I winced.

"I'm still all purple from the colloidal in the well." She showed me her arms and legs.

Her legs were the worst, a purple that almost turned blue.

"Damn, that's bad." I gasped in shock.

"Yeah, it's not painful, it's just odd." She shrugged.

"I think you should see a doctor." I laughed.

"My Dr. is a long way from here." she sighed as she thought of Jax.

"It all developed fast between you two, didn't it?" I asked.

"Sometimes it chooses you. I found him by accident, but I stayed on purpose. When you know, you know." She smiled unwillingly.

I continued to scrub the dishes in the sink and lay them on the counter to dry while we sat in a numbing silence. Lucy was hell-bent on one of two things. Finding Jax or finding her family. Only one of them I knew was worth the risk.

"At least no werewolf will touch you." I snickered.

She laughed at my joke and jiggled a set of keys.

"Can I trust you?" She questioned.

"I'm not about to defy Arthur, sorry." I muttered.

"Let me talk to them." She insisted.

"I have a debt to pay here, until they release me, I'm staying to defend them." I nodded.

"We should all be going, it's not safe here anymore. More wolves are moving north every day. Soon we'll be unable to defend the girls." Arthur interrupted from the doorway.

"Did something happen?" I asked.

"There's a lot of activity in the woods." Arthur sighed.

"Start packing." Mindy ordered as she filled an ice box with food.

"There's a lost and found down the hall with an abundance of clothes." Lucy explained as I followed her out of the kitchen.

"Lex!" Lucy called into a room.

"Shhhhh..." Lucy hissed.

My senses took over and I smelt an odor before I heard anything. Then the rats scurried through the hall and loud thumps of heavy feet pelted down on the concrete parking lot.

"They're here." I whispered.

"I'm scared." Lucy whimpered.

"Get in the bathroom, lock every door behind you." I raced to the kitchen for Arthur.

He was locking Mindy in the cool room when I laid eyes on him, and the thunderous sounds only worsened as they grew closer.

"Wolf out time." Arthur sighed as his claws grew and his hands broke seamlessly.

I hated a daytime transformation; it was never complete. It came close, but I always felt something of an anchor gripping onto my human body, I was never big enough, I was never *comfortable* in that body, not the way I was at night. Night as a werewolf was like running through the rain naked, it felt good but so forbidden, I guess that's what made it so desirable.

There was a hoard of werewolves roaming the street outside the hotel, at least twelve of them, likely more we couldn't see.

Arthur peered from the windows, ensuring we didn't set them off. If we could we had to avoid this fight, it was a fight we couldn't win even if we were more skilled than they were.

Some raced up on the buildings and vividly sniffed at the air licking at the scent eager to taste something that could lead them to another meal.

Others fought each other in the streets, throwing the dead bodies into empty shops leaving the windows stained with blood and tuffs of fur floating through the spring air. Arthur slumped against the wall and watched on longer as I stood behind a wall ready for anything.

His hair had changed over time, he was whiter now, once a dark brown, his eyes an innocent yellow. I knew Arthur had remained pure, he'd never hurt a human, and his family had kept him grounded. Not many could say the same. If I died beside him, I'd be proud of that.

He slapped me lightly as he pointed with a dagger-sharp claw.

They had a huge log with two women chained to it as other wolves stalked alongside, commanding them through the streets. The wolves walked on all fours and matched the height of those two terrified women. Alongside them they snapped and snarled fear into them, they were injured and barely able to keep up.

They were being displayed as bait for anyone brave enough to save them.

I knew we had to help them, that's what Arthur would do, it's what anyone with a conscience would do.

I looked to Arthur and let my eyes ask the question as I simpered into helplessness.

He seemed to agree as he stood tall and stretched out readying himself for something more.

I strode out on all fours; this would conceal my true size for a short time. There was something about being a non-human-eating werewolf that gave us a different size. We had more muscle, maybe it had something to do with us keeping a healthy lifestyle. Human-eating werewolves rarely had the sense to change back into humans again. Jax was the exception to the rule, he'd fed on werewolves, and this made him godly in our eyes. The Hercules of werewolves, the size he was, the strength. It couldn't be obtained on a regular diet or a human diet. That was preserved for a cannibal.

Arthur threw the doors open and the glass shattered against the walls, drawing red eyes to our direction. I walked out slowly as the other werewolves attempted to sniff us out and snap their filthy teeth at us.

I bounded for the women and lunged for the biggest wolf on the chain and tore his jaw from his skull with one swipe. I was created to fight, literally. Graham had turned me purely for this reason.

Arthur had broken the chains and the two women raced for safety.

Other wolves raced back, and a war broke out between us. I could hear Alexa breaking through the bathroom door I had barricaded her and Lucy in. But I couldn't stop them.

Alexa raced down the stairs arming herself along the way with kitchen cleavers and a meat mallet.

"Duck!" She screamed at Arthur as she launched a blade into the throat of a werewolf racing up behind him.

"STAY TOGETHER." she ordered as they surrounded the three of us.

The smaller wolves always fired first, they were more limber and could leap higher and always aimed for the neck.

One struck Arthur and latched onto his shoulder and mauled him hard and fast. Alexa used the meat mallet to hammer away at the wolf's skull as it whimpered between bites. I pulled the wolf off as it weakened and almost willingly fell off of Arthur.

Alexa was now swinging her mallet at anything within arm's reach, so I kept a good distance between us.

"LEAD THEM TO THE PRECINCT!" She ordered.

But the precinct was a pile of rubble and ash…

"The well, colloidal isn't flammable. We have to try." She urged.

"Go! NOW." she begged.

Arthur nodded to agree, and we bounded as fast as we could towards Wolftown hoping they would all follow us.

Mindy emerged with Lucy and the two girls as we raced down the street. Screams ensued and raged behind us, and then I heard Alexa's body drop to the ground and the sound of her skull being crushed in the jaws of a werewolf far bigger than her. Her spine was torn from her body, the wolf gorging himself on it as if it were a belt of candy.

Mindy lunged for the cleaver and pounded it with all her might into the back of the wolf's knee, taking it down to the ground where Lucy knelt behind it and with open hands gouged its eyes out as it writhed in pain.

"Oh fuck." one of the girls exhaled.

V.J.Garland

CHAPTER FIVE

JAX

With Ezra gone and three newbies in tow, I knew we were better off befriending them, then holding them hostage. They were as fresh as they'd get and were trainable to a degree. Untainted and most importantly embodied a desire to live, whatever that meant now.

If we didn't follow Ezra's trail, he would be the demise of the rest of the survivors.

"We follow him, but keep our distance, he can't know." I shouted as I marched back to the guys who waited anxiously outside the abandoned store.

Blue Steel was quick and eager to get in on any action and I instantly liked him. He reminded me a lot of Arthur which brought me a comfort I wasn't sure I'd know again— not in this lifetime.

"What if he smells us?" Liam asked.

"He will, but collectively we are stronger." I assured him.

"Just leave him alone, let him run wild and free." Austin yawned.

"Are you forgetting Celinde is in these same woods, she's only hours ahead of us." I growled.

"If we're lucky he'll eat everything and not turn anyone else." Rhett added.

I didn't want to admit it, but Rhett was right. That would be the best possible outcome. I was tired of fighting a battle that wasn't my own. I'd endured pain and loss at my full capacity, but I still had to function. A burnt-out werewolf was the last thing the world needed right now. Burnout was the darkest place I could be, I'd been there once before— I didn't have the people around me any longer to pull me back from that place.

We followed Ezra's trail, it was obvious, bloody, and stunk of intestinal waste.

"He's messing with us." Liam coughed.

"Typical." Austin laughed.

"Bit of a joker?" Cole asked.

"Not so much in recent years, but before that." Liam smiled.

Austin was ahead of the group picking up the trail and leading the way while I hung back with the new guys making sure they didn't stray.

"What was that?" James asked.

"That's not good…" Liam whispered.

My ears pricked up and I moved ahead of the others to join Austin.

"Werewolves?" He asked.

"A lot of them." I sighed.

"That way." I pointed towards a hill.

We had to avoid large packs. Other werewolves weren't like us, and we were outnumbered.

"When we're further away we'll use the cover of night to get over the hills." I said as I rested against a thick tree.

We were several miles away from the pack now, but still easily detectable if they caught our scent.

"Do you smell that?" Austin asked.

"What?" I asked.

"It smells like Carrie." he sighed.

"Carrie?" I glowered.

Liam raced over the hill, and I followed behind him. There was a cabin on the higher ground of the valley, and we listened intently for movement.

"Nothing." he sighed.

I smiled as we raced each other down to the porch, the door was wide open and food not too old sat in unwashed dishes on the sink in the small kitchen. The living area was messy with blankets and cushions strewn everywhere and a jacket I seemed to recognize.

"Celinde was here." I beamed.

"Isn't that Carrie's?" Liam questioned.

"Yeah, but Celinde was wearing it the day Carrie died." I explained.

"Oh." he sighed and placed it on the arm of the sofa.

The others caught up and slumped into the armchairs in the living room as I closed the door behind us.

"Two hours…" I groaned at the others as they closed their eyes and gave in to the desire to sleep.

But I couldn't sleep, not now that I knew Celinde was close, and Ezra was in between us.

Celinde was savvy, but against Ezra, she wouldn't stand a chance and she didn't know how far he'd fallen. She'd approach him as a friend and be torn to shreds before she could defend herself. The amount of food left out told me there was more than one person here with her. The shelves in the basement had faded circles where cans of food had been removed.

I packed as many cans as I could and ate bowls upon bowls of food before the others woke. It would get me through for a few more days, but places like this were going to become harder and harder to come by.

"Time to get up." I shook Austin and Liam first.

"Ugh, Jax! Just another five minutes." Liam squeezed the pillow a little tighter.

Austin ripped the pillow from his grasp and Liam's face planted on the cold solid ground.

"Dude!" Liam raised his face with a bloodied nose that healed not long after.

"Woah." Rhett observed in horror.

"You can do that too." I grinned. It was probably the only portion of being a werewolf I enjoyed – the ultra-fast healing.

"Broken bones?" James asked.

"Everything?" I shrugged slightly unsure of how lycanthropy would fare against disease.

"That's a neat trick." Cole grazed his arm with a blade from the kitchen and watched it heal.

"Ok, let's get a move on." I ordered.

I had packed as much of the food into sacks as I could and raided the supply of flares and firearms.

"Guns?" James asked.

"You never know." I sighed.

"Better to be prepared for anything." Austin patted me on the shoulder.

We kept low and moved in pairs, so we didn't make too much noise as we moved through the woods. We were still uncomfortably close to a large pack of wolves and had to keep our activity minimized.

V.J.Garland

CHAPTER SIX

CELINDE

The hospital was dark at night, there were no lights on like you would expect in a functioning hospital. Zane let me venture onto the roof, but only if he accompanied me. He had a key for every door, and I felt like a prisoner all over again.

It was distastefully dark at night for a place that was once a city. In the distance, fires still raged, and smoke blew into our faces burning our eyes as we sipped over burnt coffee.

The others seemed to keep their distance from me, I wasn't complaining. This was nothing but a bunch of misfits and aggressors, the ones you truly expected to survive a situation like this. The kind of people who only looked out for themselves and gravitated to others just like them—a simple invitation for a knife in the back.

"Not what you expected?" Zane asked as he leaned against the brick wall and the wind whipped my hair across my face.

"Which part?" I questioned.

"Werewolves' being the end of the world…" he sighed.

"I think we were all too prepared for zombies." I said with sarcasm.

"Zombies would have been better. These guys can turn back and plot." he grumbled.

"Not always." I mused.

"Tell me what you know?" He asked gently.

"I know they can become trapped in their wolf bodies if they feed too often." I sighed.

"That's good, what else?" He pressed.

"Can I trust you?" A tear escaped my already burning eyes.

"Yes." he nodded.

"You won't like what I'm about to tell you and you may very well throw me over the edge of the building and I'd be okay with that." I winced.

"What's so bad?" He moved closer to me.

"I don't think I am anymore, but during the blood moon I was able to turn also, I wasn't in control of myself. So, I know what it's like to be a victim of this madness. I've been scratched more times than I can count." I rolled up my shirt and showed him my plethora of wounds from my own stupidity of attempting to break up a brawl that once broke out in the precinct.

"I've never seen a female turn." He was puzzled.

"We don't, we hibernate in our human bodies for a hundred years apparently, and then we go back to normal." I sniffed.

"So, you're healed?" He beamed.

"For another hundred years, I think." I nodded.

"I see." he sighed.

"If you need to lock me away that's okay." I submitted my defeat.

"I trust you. I don't think I need to do that, but if you know how to stop this, I need you to cooperate with me." he pleaded.

I sighed heavily as I knew what I was about to say couldn't be taken back, but I was tired. I was tired of endless nights and dreary days, looking over my shoulder and my friends dying. I didn't recognize the person I'd become. And in that moment of weakness, it felt right to betray them. I'd tell Zane how to destroy them because I wanted my old life back. I wanted a world of Starbucks and burgers, movie nights, and cocktails. I wanted them dead—all of them.

"Go to every pharmacy you can find and take all of the colloidal silver you can get your hands on. It won't be enough but it's a start. And water guns." I added.

"Colloidal?" He asked.

"It burns through their skin fast and gets stuck in their veins between healings. I had a friend who lived with trace amounts of it, he was in chronic pain. It wasn't enough to kill him, but it *can* kill them if you have enough." I sighed at the thought of Tristan.

Zane ran down the stairs to the others and I followed behind him.

"EVERYONE UP!" He ordered as he entered the sleeping quarters.

"We're rolling out, we need to hit every pharmacy and collect every bottle of colloidal silver you can find." He was on a mission.

He grasped my wrist and took me aside.

"Stay here." he ordered as he brushed past me.

"Zane, I can help." I argued.

"You just did." he smiled.

I had just signed a death warrant for all my friends out there, but I had lost remorse for their cause—they didn't have one anymore.

Zane and the others loaded up into their trucks and set out into the deserted city. Lincoln and I were the only ones left behind.

"Coffee?" Lincoln asked.

"Got anything stronger?" I asked.

"That's a girl!" He smacked me on the back and chuckled.

He led me to the kitchen and pulled out a bottle of rum from a cupboard and poured us each a full glass.

"You got this." He winked as he sipped at his glass.
I wasn't trying to get drunk, but I really did need to take the edge off.

"Zane will never know; you'll be passed out before their back." he laughed.

"Bottoms up." I shrugged my shoulders.

I chugged a third of the glass surprisingly well and propped myself up on the bench as I watched Lincoln comb through bags of MREs.

"What's for supper?" I glowered as I examined ugly green and brown bags of overly processed food.

"Looking like hard tack and coffee, just for something different." he teased.

I ripped open a bag of hard tack and soaked one of the hard crackers in my rum before eating it.

"Damn!" Lincoln said squeamishly.

"You're going to see worse than that in the months to come." I assured him.

"You seem to be well in the depths of it already?" He asked.

"Years." I was exasperated as I felt the effects of the rum. I was at the end of the glass before I knew it as I snacked on the soggy-tack biscuits and made light banter with Lincoln about how much we despised Zeek. Then we heard a loud growl shaking the gates that had been recently erected to protect the building.

We stumbled out and into the ambulance bay as we observed two of the trucks with a large werewolf chained between them and a dark hessian sack soaked in colloidal covering its head. The werewolf bled from the neck down as silver played on his skin.

"Get it into the psych ward, we can restrain it there." Zane ordered.

Mateo and some others I hadn't met had rebar poles with chains welded onto the ends forcing the wolf into the direction of their choosing.

"Where did you find that one?" I asked slightly impressed by its size. I hadn't seen a werewolf of this size since I left Wolftown.

"He was munching on a pack of dead wolves behind a restaurant." Zane answered.

"He was alone?" I asked.

"Yep." he replied.

"Sorry, but you reek of alcohol!" he laughed as he held his nose.

"Yeah, Lincoln got me hammered on the rum-rocked hard tack." I poked my tongue at him childishly.

"Okay, off to bed. I have a werewolf to interrogate." He nudged me up the stairs.

"I should come, I'm experienced!" I winked.

"You're drunk…" He crossed his arms.

"Let's be real, I probably should be for this." I raised my arms and batted my eyes at him as I felt my body tingle from the alcohol.

"Let her join in." Lincoln came to my aid.

"Fine but stay back!" Zane agreed reluctantly and his eyes narrowed at me with his serious words.

We crept down the stairs to a hallway of rooms with doors that led to more doors and windows. Rooms with restraints and one now newly decorated with chains and a small selection of weapons outside the door. I armed myself with a water gun and poured in a bottle of the colloidal Zane had returned with.

"I'm going first!" I slammed the door behind me darting past the others as they secured the massive werewolf to metal links bored deeply into the foundation of the hospital.

I tore the sack from the head of the werewolf and sat on the floor a good distance away. The room was mostly dark, the only light coming from the window in the door, and Zane's body blocked out a lot of it as he watched on eagerly.

"Turn!" I demanded.

If I was going to get anything from this beast, I needed him to be able to speak, I needed his human form. He was no good to me as a werewolf.

"We can do this the easy way or the painful way." I pumped the water gun, so I had a stream ready to fire.

Zane watched through the window ordering me with his eyes to keep back.

The werewolf growled and slumped and hung from the chains in pain from the burns on his face.

"Come on…" I pressed.

He growled once more and fell to his knees but still not obeying.

"Pew pew!" I shot at his torso with my colloidal leaving burns over his chest playfully.

A roar left his body, and he slowly became smaller and his presence less intimidating.

"Good, where did you come from?" I grunted. His face was a melty burnt mess and glimmers of light that bounced off the silver that glowed from his burns that were now clinging to his bones.

"North." He coughed. His face was badly welted from the burns. His lips seemed to almost merged together as he tried to speak through the pain. The room was still too dark to make out a face if that were even possible.

"Were there others with you?" I asked.

"Not for a long time." He huffed.

Zane moved and a glimmer of light filled the room and I immediately felt sober as I recognized the tattoos on the body before me.

"EZRA!" I screamed as I raced to support his suspended body.

"NO, GET BACK!" He roared with barely any self-control. It wasn't a human roar. It was a wolf roar, and I knew he was gone. The beast had taken him.

"Celinde, I didn't think I'd see you again." His kind, cheeky smile escaped through the one good side of his lips.

"What did they do to you?" I cried.

Zane cracked the door and came in behind me and pulled me further away, but I fought him as I pushed him away.

"No! He's, my friend." I cried.

"Open your eyes, do you see what's in front of you? This creature isn't your friend, he will kill you if you let down your guard." Zane scowled as he held my arms down beside me.

"We were attacked by another group of wolves, I did what I had to, to protect the others. You were already across the river. They would have caught you." Ezra explained.

Words failed me but my expression was telling, Ezra was the only reason I got away alive.

Zane's arms loosened around me as he felt my weight shift from rage to sadness.

"Carrie wouldn't want this for you." I cried.

"And Christian would want you to put me out of my misery, please Celinde. Give me mercy, I don't want to live like this anymore, there's no redemption for me." He cried.

"I can't take your life." I wiped my tears as Zane left the room trusting me.

"What's left for us after this, there's no more Precinct. I'm done Cel. Please…" He begged.

But I couldn't utter anything, it all seemed so nonsensical. This wasn't how it was supposed to end. Yet I knew the end was close the day I told Zane what would help us win this fight. I had aligned myself with humans after years of helping the enemy.

"Aren't you tired of this life?" He questioned.

I was lost for words as I nodded and fell to my knees as I agreed to his request to end his suffering. The door opened behind me, and Zane held my shoulder and gave it a gentle squeeze.

"Take care of her…" Ezra gasped. He entrusted me to Zane with one exchange of words.

"I will." Zane swept a surgical saw across Ezra's throat and went back three times more to hack the head from the body as I clambered onto the floor screaming as I slipped in the blood trying to pull myself to Ezra's body.

"Celinde…" Zane pulled me from one side as I fought him slipping in the large heap of blood. I clung to Ezra's corpse in desperation. His head was in Zane's hand, held up by Ezra's long natural dreadlocked hair.

"LEAVE ME!!" I screamed.

I was soaked in Ezra's blood now, but I didn't care. I wailed and cried as if nobody could see me, but Zane waited outside the door for all the hours I lay in the puddle of grief that consumed me.

It was the moment I truly absorbed everything that had happened through the years. The loss, the abandonment, the innocent people who died or worse, lived a life alongside this chaos. I had only wished Lupe took all of us out when she went after the Precinct. That was power, knowing, owning the position, and still having the strength to do the right thing for the greater well-being of others even though she would perish with them.

Zane came into the room as I slipped between consciousness and sleep. He collected me into his arms and carried me up the stairs. Lincoln and the others were in the halls with a look of remorse in their eyes as they showered me in their pity or judged me. Zane took me up to our room and sat me in the corner of the shower as the water ran and he sat with me as I clawed at him desperate for him to be someone I recognized, someone who could take the pain away and mask my agony.

"I'm so sorry." He grasped my wrists softly and held my eyes in his. They were full of empathy and regret.

"You only did as he asked." I sighed as I watched all the blood spin into the vent.

"I took your friend though. Celinde, I owe you a debt. Whatever you want, whatever you need, I'll do it." He stroked my cheek.

"Help me make the world right again." I sighed.

"Whatever it takes…" He moved closer and held my hands as my head spun. I sunk into his warm embrace and wept as I accepted he was the closest thing to a friend I'd have for next lifetime to come.

Hunter's Moon: Caged

V.J.Garland

Chapter Six

Lucy

Mindy was wrestling the blind werewolf on the ground as Arthur and Evan disappeared towards the Precinct.

"Lucy! GET THAT LOG." she meant the same log the other girls had been tied to.

I raced to the log and hauled it over to Mindy with the chains Alexa had punished Evan with and together we forced the log down the throat of the werewolf. It was just thin enough to make it through his jaws and neck, and we were hopeful this would disable it long enough for us to get away, but at the same time ensure absolute suffering for what his group had done to Alexa.

"I need to bury my daughter..." Mindy was numb, bloodied, and in a trance like state.

Mindy gripped Alexa by the hood of her jacket and with strength only a grieving mother could muster she dragged her body down the street one hundred meters or so across the road into a clearing that once resembled a children's play space.

I followed behind with the two others. Their feet were blistered, red, and bruised, but they still pushed through.

In a sandpit, there was a child's trowel, a bucket, and a toy truck with a weathered doll in the tray.

"Mindy..." I whispered softly.

But she didn't utter a word in response. She never made eye contact with me, she simply collected the trowel and began digging in the sandpit.

I kneeled beside her and raked my hands through the sand, the others soon joined us. Our hands were weak and achy by then of the digging. It didn't take us long to get through the sand layer, it was the earth layer that made it work, but we collectively managed to dig a shallower-than-usual grave.

"This was my only child…" Mindy's eyes glazed over with tears as she spoke softly, stroking Alexa's face for the final time.

"I hope you girls never feel how it feels to bury a child." She cried.

I stepped back with the others and sat in the grass to allow Mindy the time she needed to say goodbye.

Mindy lay beside Alexa, cuddling what warmth she still had, the hoodie of her jacket the only thing keeping her head intact to her body.

 Dust began to hover past the clouds and darkened the park and town further. I edged gently towards Mindy and pulled her up and out from her sorrow—her face puffy and red. I wrapped my arms around her, and she wailed one last time. That support gave her one last burst of energy to feel all the loss and completely let herself go.

Her scream was enough to break me. It was a scream that resonated with what true heartbreak felt like. The sound of your heart leaving your body to join the body that once gave you meaning. That was the numbness I felt. Mindy's once joyful and bright essence had left her body. Her reason for living, fighting, and simply being, was now gone, decaying within Alexa's body. The universe had stolen her favourite person and turned her into a lesson.

The other two girls graciously moved over and helped us as I lifted Alexa's legs and Mindy supported her head. They grabbed an arm each and we all placed Alexa gently into the grave. The wind swept the first layer of dirt back into the hole. I grabbed the trowel and scattered sand and earth over the body as Mindy stood back unable to compose herself for a final glimpse at Alexa as the rest of us did our best to cover the body.

The sky was brighter tonight. It shone a path towards the outskirts of town to the road that led to the Precinct and my eyes locked with Mindy's as I asked questions in my own mind about whether or not we should be taking that path.

But why not? Was there really a road that led to safety and warm beds anymore? It didn't matter which direction I took, all that waited for us was destruction, and nowhere to hide. So, I took the brightened path. Tonight, I'd run with the wolves.

The wolves I trusted and hoped had survived the onslaught that other wolves would bring.

"What are your names?" I asked the others.

"Giselle." One raised her hand. She was a college student and looked paler than a ghost, in need of a good meal and a week's worth of sleep.

"I'm Eden." the other replied.

Eden was taller, with dark features, longer hair braided back down to her lower back, she was covered in scrapes and bruises. Giselle was short, only five feet with electric green eyes so light they shouldn't be real. She had long dark hair also, but hers was out and matted from what I could only assume was days of torment if not longer.

"I'm Lucy, that's Mindy." I sighed as I looked towards Mindy.

They were curious about me, about my skin and I sunk into an immediate confession like word vomit.

"I was in a well for too long with a chemical, it stained my skin." I said with some embarrassment.

"Don't be embarrassed, none of us are looking our best." Giselle smiled as she pointed to her feet.

"Let's see if we can find you some shoes." I pointed to the abandoned Costco a few blocks down.

"Good idea." Mindy shouted as she cocked a gun and then pulled herself out of a window to the gun store and handed us one each.

Mindy wasn't one to succumb to defeat, she would avenge Alexa if it were the last thing she did, and she'd gladly give her life in the process. She always gave one hundred percent of herself, I admired that about her, but I worried how she'd respond in her current state.

We walked through the darkness down the street into Costco with nothing but the moonlight guiding us. The doors were wide open, the shelves mostly untouched except for the now rotting produce and water.

"Only take what we need, we can't carry a lot." Mindy ordered.

We looked through the footwear for sturdy hiking boots, thick clothing, hiking equipment, and anything that might be useful. Mindy was filling backpacks with shelf-stable foods and spare socks and underwear.

"Lucy?" Giselle called from a few aisles over.

"Coming." I replied as I followed her voice.

Eden was on top of a ride on lawn mower and Giselle on another.

"Beats walking?" She smiled as she pointed to two more.

"Mindy?" I yelled as I entertained the idea.

"Oh! Load them up." Mindy dumped the bags on top of one.

Giselle was quite handy; she began fixing baskets to the front ends of each mower and filled them with supplies.

"Leave that one empty for fuel." I ordered as I heaved jerry cans into it.

"We should get going, Evan and Arthur might need us." I tried to wrangle the others together.

"Agreed." Mindy climbed up onto her mower and we drove them all out to the petrol station and filled the mowers and cans as much as we could.

Mindy stopped us to wait for her as she backtracked to the werewolf who murdered Alexa. He was still alive, barely. She climbed down and removed the log; she lay one final kick into its body and then she climbed up onto her mower and revved the blades and ran over the werewolf multiple times until he resembled nothing more than ground meat.

She drove back splattered in blood and nodded to move forward.

"She would have loved that." I smiled.

"She would have." She agreed as we switched on the torches we had attached and drove into the darkness.

The mowers will get us there on one tank of fuel and hopefully out with whatever we had stored in the jerry cans.

It was odd being so close and so exposed but so ready. My gun slung over my shoulder, a knife in my leg pocket, and a water gun ready to be filled from the well if worst case scenario was what we were about to walk into.

"Be on your guard, they'll hear us before we hear them." Mindy advised Giselle and Eden.

"Don't turn on your blades till you've made contact, we need to preserve the fuel as long as we can." I added.

"You guys have been doing this a while haven't you?" Giselle asked.

"Sadly." Mindy answered.

"Her longer than me." I sighed.

Mindy was the mother and master of our group even if nobody said it. Without Mindy the wheels of Wolftown simply did not spin. Jax thought so highly of her and spoke to me often about how he had let her, and Carrie do their thing without his interference.

The closer we got the more I felt his presence. I knew he wasn't there, but the hope brought me some comfort.

It was the comfort of his touch, but mostly the knowledge that werewolves had a chance to rehabilitate. It was a long shot, but it was the glimmer of hope I needed to keep me going, if only for one more night.

We smelt the smoke first, then saw the orange of the flames, and soon felt the heat from the aggressive flickering from the flames. It was the outer perimeters that were ablaze. From high on the hill, I could see Evan and Arthur with bodies piled around them looking physically spent, but still more wolves standing, all of them drenched in blood.

Mindy pressed her foot on the gas harder and burst through a clearing only *just* wide enough for the mowers to fit. She turned on her blades. Stood on the mower and fired her gun at the pack of wolves. Three raced towards her, but Giselle followed Mindy's lead, set her blades abuzz, stood and let her thighs drive the mower, and took aim at the closest werewolf. Mindy took out the first wolf and crushed its skull in her blades, the mower leaping as if it went over a mound of earth.

Evan and Arthur howled in excitement. Our presence seemed to give them the final jolt they needed to carry on.

Eden and I joined Mindy and Giselle and made a beeline towards the well. I roped off the water guns and dropped them into the well and filled them with what colloidal I could reach.

A wolf chased after me and I flicked the rope saturated in the liquid silver death and it backed away cautiously. I raised the guns and crossed them over my body as I aimed one at the wolf with intimidation. He was far bigger than me and skulked around ready to pounce as I tested him with shots that burnt at his face.

"Come on fucker!" I growled.

The werewolf licked his muzzle as he stood on two legs, showing off his size as he attempted to intimidate me. Eden raced to my side, and I tossed her a gun of colloidal.

"Let's go." She was amped and excitable with a dangerous streak of fearlessness now flooding her veins.

We fired as more wolves circled, they were intrigued, but hungrier. After all, what were two little girls going to do to this one big werewolf?

"FIRE!" I shouted. We emptied our guns into the crowd of them.

The single large wolf still giving fight. I pulled my dagger and ran to bury it in his face, but he caught me in his jaws and sunk his teeth into my arm. Shock took over first before I realized he had quickly spat me back out. He was weakened immediately and began to turn back into a human as the burn melted the flesh from his face.

Mindy raced to my side to compress my bleeding as I watched on in horror.

"He's allergic to you!" Giselle exasperated.

"Your skin." Mindy nodded as she agreed with Giselle.

Evan and Arthur tore through the remaining wolves while Eden used a mower to ensure they weren't coming back in a hurry.

"Kill him!" Mindy ordered Giselle.

She threw her my gun to finish off the wolf who had bitten me.

"I'm sorry." She closed her eyes and unloaded the remains of the gun into the throat of the already suffering wolf.

His eyes became cloudy as his life left him. Giselle in pieces as she collapsed onto his body in shock.

The rest were barely alive, Eden was doing a good job of finishing them off, and Evan sat beside me as Mindy did what she could to stop my arm bleeding. He had barely sunk in his fangs before my toxic blood began to poison him.

"Good job Lucy." Evan nudged.

"I didn't do that on purpose." I groaned.

"Regardless, it worked and weakened the rest with doubt." He sighed.

"Are you alright?" Arthur asked as he rubbed Mindy's shoulder.

"I'll be okay." I nodded. My eyes drifted to Mindy who was still a beacon of hope, a warrior, but one suffering from an illness worse than any other— grief.

"You guys did good with the mowers." Evan applauded.

"I think mine is busted." Eden jumped down as she parked near us to check on Giselle.

"It served its purpose." Arthur acknowledged.

Eden pulled Giselle up and wiped the tears off her face.

"You're going to be okay!" Eden slapped her shoulders and hugged her.

As Mindy sutured the bite marks on my arm closed with a sewing kit as I watched the others. Eden was strong for someone her size; she packed a punch. Giselle was brave but full of compassion.

Arthur was between two minds, he knew Alexa had suffered a fatal attack and he was wracked with sadness, but also joy that the same wolves didn't take the love of his life. Mindy had carried the weight of Alexa's death though, leaving her as nothing more than a shell of the person she had been before. Arthur had a lot of catching up to do.

Evan sat with his head between his legs, every so often looking up and observing Eden and Giselle.

"Let's see if we can salvage that mower." He jumped up and offered his hand out to Giselle. Eden was already on her feet and cleaning herself off.

"I'm Evan." He smiled.

Their exchange was fluid and sweet, she took an interest in him, and I had no concerns. If a romance is what kept him human, I was on his side. I had once been that reason for Jax. I missed him. I knew I would probably never see him again, not in this life, and if we did cross paths again, it was likely destined to be short-lived.

I promised myself in this moment I wouldn't live my life grasping for more, I'd appreciate all the small moments.

Mindy was done and wrapped my arm in a bandage and sling.

"Pump out as much of that as we can." Mindy pointed to the well as she gave orders to Arthur.

"Where are we going?" I asked.

"To find our family, we should have never separated." She sighed.

"They could be anywhere." Evan interrupted.

"Well, just as well you have a nose that can sniff Jax out." Mindy growled.

"Wait, what if he's dead?" I asked.

"If Jax is dead I would be too." Arthur added.

"Huh? How?" Giselle questioned.

"Jax was our leader, we're bonded to his fate if you will." Arthur explained.

"So, what does that mean?" I asked.

"If he dies, I die. That's how it happened for Noah, Wesley, Graham, even Jerry." he added.

"That's unfortunate." Giselle sighed.

"That's how I know he's alive." Arthur smiled.

"Well let's get moving." I was excited and exhausted all in the same breath.

"We might need an alternative mode of transportation. These aren't going to get us too far." Evan sighed as he concluded that the fourth mower was broken.

"We still have three until we find something else." Arthur said as he climbed on with Mindy.

"Buddie's?" Evan smiled at Giselle. She blushed and held onto the back of him once aboard the mower he had saddled.

"Come on, Eden." I reached my hand to help her onto the mower and she accepted.

"I have a scent, there's a huge movement of werewolves going south." Arthur said as he drove towards the border.

"Let's go, they'll be following them." I raced faster south.

We were in for days, maybe even weeks of rough traveling. Not just traveling but hiding *and* surviving.

V.J.Garland

CHAPTER SEVEN

JAX

If we weren't silent, we'd never survive the onslaught of werewolves *or* humans. We didn't have the numbers for a full-fledged war. The new guys had little to no experience and were only just piecing it all together as they went. Granted they would survive far longer with us and remain in a more human-like state.

As we moved closer to towns on the East Coast, I could hear the interference of radios desperately seeking communication with others— It had become a wasteland.

You could barely move five miles without seeing or smelling a decaying body. Where there were bodies, there were werewolves, and there were bodies everywhere.

Ezra's scent became harder to track as we entered a town that I could no longer recognize but knew to be Philadelphia. It had been raided by humans from top to bottom. Windows smashed, doors unhinged, and the blood— there was so much blood.

It was almost a relief to see a single werewolf body dead and crushed by a weakened foundation, glass from a window impalement leading it to have bled out. A good sign that there were other ways we could die.

"There's nobody here." James whispered.

"Find cover for the night." I ordered.

Lucy was out there somewhere, hopefully safe, and away from the chaos that now ruled the world. Thoughts of her often played in my mind, but I was quick to shut them down. The unknown was a torment I couldn't afford to entertain distractions.

"In here." Austin tapped me on the arm.

It was an old sports bar, with bench seats good enough to sleep on for a night, even if our legs would be hanging off the ends.

"Any beer?" Liam grumbled.

"No beer, but there's this." Rhett tossed him a bottle of whiskey.

"That'll keep me warm." Liam held it to his chest with affection in his grin.

"You're sharing that." James raised an eyebrow as he looked through a shelf of empty bottles.

"Sure." Liam replied reluctantly.

"You really need a girlfriend." Austin laughed.

"Yes, well if you come across a live woman who likes me during my monthlies, I'll take her." he said with a sarcastic tone.

We'd been at this long enough now that we were able to control our transformations just enough to sleep.

It all came down to our moods. Most of us were able to sleep in both forms, but it wasn't advised. With humans now hunting us, we were an immediate threat if we appeared as werewolves. As humans, we could evade both species to some degree with added measures of caution. We couldn't always be choosy with who we attacked—unless there was a greater antagonist to be sought.

The nights leading up to this point seemed to drag on. They weren't silent and peaceful anymore. They were full of activity, restlessness, growling, and fighting between our species over food. Soon the main food source would run out. Another month like this and there'd be no humans left to eat. The pack we'd seen was heavily populated with werewolves who had overindulged and gorged themselves stupidly on human bodies. What was left was of no interest to them while they were frenzied and chaotic. The doomsday prepper's stashes would be useless, they'd be left untouched. No door would stand the brute force of a hungry werewolf, and a hungry werewolf could smell over miles and through barriers of any kind.

When the bodies run out, there's only each other, that's when the real problems will begin. Ezra was one of my closest confidants, one of the strongest werewolves I'd ever come across and he could barely fight the urge to give into his carnal instincts.

When I went down the same darkened path it was like a red glaze hovered over my eyes. Everything and everyone were a potential meal. The willpower it took—it would have been easier to give in.

There are still days I wish I did. Maybe if the others had put me down, we could have avoided all of this, but I knew the real cause—Jerry.

Jerry's one night of fun on Hurricane Ridge had an explosive domino effect, granted it was delayed years, but all it took was one werewolf—one werewolf and the world died.

I wasn't the problem, not the way I had punished myself into believing all of these years. Wesley was a different evil; he was the devil's advocate.

My mind was constantly buzzing with thoughts of the past. It was getting harder to remember Joel, I had no pictures of him. What I remembered was his cheekiness, his excitement, and his passion to live life on the edge, no matter how high or steep that edge was.

All the things I remembered about Lupe barely made sense anymore, it was as if she was two different people. In one life she was this incredibly frail, broken woman. In the next, she was strong, full of rage, determined to decimate our kind, but she was dead and embodied all the things she had once hated, and it was clear she hated herself. I wasn't stupid, I smelt blood on her, and so did Noah. She hadn't been strong enough to resist the urge, maybe that's what drove her to that final moment when she ignited the Precinct into flurries of hot red embers.

I wish I had one last hour with her, just to ask her what went through her mind, to tell it was okay one last time.

The others slept on the benches as I watched out from the cracks between the boards that covered the windows, they were covered in old wood that splintered my nose every time I almost dozed off, a violent reminder I had a job to do.

My eyes felt like they were bulging out of my head. I'd had hardly any sleep since we left that sweet little mansion and enjoyed beers with my closest and dearest for the last time. Had I known, I wouldn't have been in any hurry to leave.

"Guys." I shrugged Liam first.

"Everyone up, there's a tank coming." I explained as I heard old cars grind beneath their tracks.

The city was a mess, the streets impassable for vehicles. They were buried in rumble from explosions, cars abandoned, the streets painted in blood.

"Do we go out there?" Liam asked.

"Act as human as you can." I sighed with hesitation.

"You sure about this?" Austin asked.

"Can you hold it together?" I asked as I looked at Rhett, James, and Cole.

"We got this." Rhett spoke for them all.

"Okay, let's go." I pushed the doors open as the tank approached the bar.

The hatch opened and a man peered through with a gun aimed at me.

"Take it easy, we're friendly." I lied.

"You sure?" He asked.

"Oh, come on. He can speak! Isn't that enough." Another man pushed a door open as he yelled up to the man in the hatch.

"Yeah, I guess so." He chuckled as he lowered his weapon.

They all climbed out of the tank and greeted us.

"I'm Zane, this is Getty, that's Max." he pointed to the driver.

"Jax." I shook his hand.

"Where you headed?" Zane asked.

"Anywhere." I shrugged my shoulders.

"We're gearing up to head to Manhattan, it's been declared safe, if we can get there." He explained.

"Are you army?" I asked.

"Marines." He pointed to himself and Getty.

"I'm Navy." Max answered.

"You?" Zane was curious.

"No, a surgeon." I replied.

"We're having some luck lately." He smiled.

"Oh?" I questioned.

"We just found another straggler, a paramedic, but she's in no shape to be caring for anyone. She needs the care." Zane sighed.

I knew exactly who he was talking about, but I didn't know how much she had told him, I didn't know if my words were safe.

"You're welcome to join us, we could use the extra help, you look like a strong bunch." Zane was looking over the others in approval.

"We'll follow you." I nodded.

Zane walked alongside us as Max and Getty drove back to their base, a run-down hospital with multiple layers of fencing around it, scaffolds erected into watch towers and the odd soldier pacing the fence line.

"Where are we?" I asked as I looked around unable to recognize the cityscape.

"Philadelphia." Zane confirmed my suspicions.

"Shit, we made it that far." Liam said excitably.

"Where did you come from?" Zane asked.

"Tennessee." I lied.

I looked back at the others and with a glare, I ordered lies and dishonesty.

I didn't want to lie, but we weren't safe. There would likely be more of these guys, marines were the kind of guys who always stuck together.

"Just over here." Zane led us.

We walked all the way around the hospital to the one singular entry. It was wrapped in barbed wire and had gates just big enough for the tanks to roll into the hot zone of the hospital. The hot zone was full of ransacked ambulances, most without tires now.

It was evident that parts of the hospital had been looted before it was turned into a base.

We followed the tank through the gates where other soldiers opened the gates and welcomed us in.

In the corner of my eye, I spied Celinde shying away behind the corner. Liam saw her too and almost burst out of his skin, I grabbed his arm and held him back trying not to act too obvious.

"We don't know what she's told them, we can't act familiar." I whispered.

Austin looked on in disapproval as Celinde swallowed a large gulp. I could hear her heart pumping faster; I could feel the warmth radiating off her skin as she became flushed with fear.

Zane introduced us to some others hovering about drinking coffee and smoking cigarettes in the kitchen.

"We'll be leaving here once all this food is used up." He explained.

Celinde followed us into the kitchen, disguising her curiosity for thirst as she reached into a Yeti cooler for a bottle of water.

"Celinde is our resident medic." Zane smiled.

"Nice to meet you, I'm Jax." my throat became raspy.

Her better judgment failed her as she lunged in to hug me, and Zane became wary.

I knew she must have said something, but *what?*

"You know each other?" Zane interrupted what was now becoming an awkwardly long hug.

"Sorry, you just remind me of someone." She lied as she wiped tears from her cheeks.

Zane was protective of her, and aching thoughts rushed through my mind of what she may have done to survive here.

I exchanged a familiar look with her, and her honest eyes confirmed her safety. I felt relief instantly, Christian would never forgive me if I let harm come to her, but the real harm was me.

"You must be dying for a shower." She said as she tried to lighten the mood.

"Two minutes each, wet yourselves, turn it off, scrub, then rinse, we're almost out of water." Lincoln ordered as he pointed us to a trolley of hospital towels.

Zane led us down a hallway to an old surgical room that now doubled as a bedroom.

"You can use this room." He said as he pushed the door open.

"Thanks." I entered the room and closed the door after everyone had entered.

The room was a stale white, covered in an off-yellow soot from all the smoke. The windows had been left open during the first of the attacks and were shattered but still intact from the protective layer of plastic.

To the side of the room was a pile of dirty clothes, another pile of clean linens, and another pile of wet bloodied linens. Further along two poorly made beds adjacent to one another.

One end of the room had an accessible bathroom, one of those ones where the shower bleeds into the rest of the room, a tap with no cupboards, only a plastic-style mirror, the ones that dulled over time and became nothing but a ghostly reflection.

"Shotgun!" Austin grabbed a towel and raced for the shower.

"She's not okay, somethings up with her." Liam groaned with concern.

"Rhett, Cole, James, stay here." I nodded to Liam as we left the room and walked the halls.

We had hardly gone a hundred feet when we heard Celinde crying in a closet. I tore the door open, and she cowered inside almost in fear of me.

"What did they do to you?" I asked as I reached for her.

"Nothing, they haven't touched me." She cried.

Liam leaned in and met her level as he pulled her to him.

"I'm so sorry." She wailed.

"It's okay, we found you." I brushed her hair back as I sat on the ground with them.

"Ezra…" Her eyes filled with tears and welled there a moment too long until she forced them away with a blink.

"You've seen him?" I asked.

"You can't lose your shit Jax." She held my face in her hands and a seriousness crossed her.

"What did you do?" I questioned.

"It was what he wanted; you know he wouldn't want to live like that." She pressed harder into my face forgetting her own strength.

"Celinde, tell us what happened?" Liam pulled her hands away from my face.

"He's dead." she dropped her face into her palms as she cried some more.

"WHO?" Liam was furious.

"No, Liam. He wanted this." Celinde tore at Liam's arm as he stood tall and staunchly ready for murder.

"Explain…" I grasped her wrists.

"He was caught when the marines went out patrolling, he had smelt my scent, Carrie's jacket I suppose. They locked him in one of the psych rooms and they knew I had some experience with werewolves, and they let me interrogate him. Jax, I swear I didn't even recognize him; his face was so badly burnt from the colloidal that it had melted his skin. It wasn't until I got him to turn, that I saw his tattoos and I stopped." She took a deep breath.

"You told them about the colloidal?" Liam growled.

"In case you haven't noticed I'm surrounded by humans and there's an army of werewolves out there likely to attack us any day, so yeah! I told them how we can protect ourselves, if it comes down to it Liam, I choose my species over yours!" She screamed.

"Yours?" Zane's voice echoed in the halls.

"Fuck." I sighed.

"You aren't human? I knew that hug was too meaningful. Big brother?" Zane cocked a gun and aimed it at my head.

"We aren't like them; we can help you." I grasped the gun and bent the length of it.

He dropped the gun and crossed his arms and stood beside Celinde.

"Why would you help *me*?" Zane asked.

"Because we don't like this either, that group of werewolves is too big, they are *too* hungry. Nothing will sustain them at this rate and then they'll turn on each other and that will be a far bigger problem." I explained.

"Well, shouldn't we just let them kill each other?" Zane questioned.

"That would be too easy." Liam laughed.

"Cannibalism in werewolves has another supernatural effect, the werewolf doing the eating will become bigger, unstoppable." She pointed me at.

"You?" Zane asked.

"There was an incident a few years ago, it was the only way to stop this developing the way it has now." I sighed as I brushed the scars on my arms from Wesley's pets.

"So, you can stop this?" Zane asked.

"No, there's too many of them, apparently you've seen what that *lifestyle* does to a werewolf?" I hinted at Ezra.

"I'm sorry about your friend. Now that you mention it though, he was huge, the biggest I've ever seen." Zane thought aloud.

"He must have had a feast on the way in, he was no bigger than me the last I saw him." I said.

"I don't need a demo, but how big are you?" Zane became curious.

"About ten feet tall. The rest of us hover around eight feet." Liam said excitedly.

"Even eight feet is a lot when humans are averaging five to six feet." Zane sighed.

"How big was Ezra?" Liam asked Celinde.

"I didn't see, he was hunched over, he was too tall for the room he was in." She answered.

"He was at least eight, maybe even up to nine feet." Zane nodded.

"He was out of control when I left him, but not that big." I added.

"Well, we better stop this from happening to anyone else, can your guys be trusted?" I asked.

"No." Celinde barked.

"Ummmm, maybe Lincoln, Mateo, and Max can be trusted, but not Zeek or Getty, best not to say anything to the others either." Zane agreed.

"Well, we need to prepare. How much colloidal do you have?" I asked.

"Here?" Zane questioned.

"If Manhattan truly is safe you don't want to bring a war to the survivors, let's have this out here." I suggested.

"Ok, we have about four drums of colloidal, we need to be smart with it." Zane said.

"Four isn't enough." Liam's eyes widened.

"It's all we've got." Celinde sighed.

"We'll leave the safe zone and check some other places." I suggested.

"I'll come." Zane nodded.

"So, no shower?" Liam grunted.

"Not today." I slapped him on the back.

"Check the bottles, they should have their manufacturers listed, if we can get to a factory…" Celinde began.

"All we need is a few fire trucks." I smiled.

"Fresh out of firefighters though." Liam added.

"Christian taught me a few things." Celinde chimed in.

"Me too." I agreed with her.

Celinde and Liam went to check the empty bottles and found the only manufacturer on the east coast.

"That's bad." Celinde said as she walked back to us.

"Where is it?" Zane sighed.

"Florida." Liam huffed.

"Up for a run?" He smiled as Austin and the rest of our guys found us in the corridor.

"What?" Austin asked.

"There's a colloidal factory, in Florida." I added.

"Okay let's go." Austin was always ready for the next challenge.

"Don't tell them how far we are going, we'll be back before you know it." I hugged Celinde and Liam along with Austin squeezed us a little too hard as they joined in. "Stay here and look after her." I zoned in on Zane.

Zane shook my hand as he pulled Celinde away, still a little unsure of us.

We walked out of the gates until we were out of sight, and we all morphed into our beasts and sprinted as fast as we could south to Florida.

V.J.Garland

CHAPTER EIGHT

ARTHUR

We'd found a truck in good working order in Calgary and fitted it with snowploughs. Eden was quite handy and even fitted the mower blades onto every side so that they'd still rotate on their own. They wouldn't function at the same speed as a mower, but they still rolled and if a werewolf got caught in it, the weight would spin them through the rotation and injure them just enough to get them off our trail.

Another two days and we made it as far as Missouri, the worst part was stopping for fuel, that was an exercise none of us liked, but every gas station had enough dead bodies and the odd loaded guns for us to protect ourselves if the situation called for it. The sight of bodies was truly the worst of it.

Hundreds if not thousands of mauled bodies littered the highways where people had stopped to defend themselves.

The truck was doing a good job of shovelling everything off to the sides, but it slowed the drive significantly when we reached the more built-up areas.

Evan was well on his way to being the best possible version of himself, he would hunt around the stores for food when everyone else was too afraid. He'd load up on supplies and ensure the girls were cared for and we took turns in driving when I was too exhausted—he was carrying more than his own weight.

He wasn't a big talker; I could sense his guilt, painted in every expression—he carried so much.

Giselle seemed to be the one who could put a smile on his face. Eden was all business, she had revenge on her mind, and her feet were so poorly she struggled to walk some days. Mindy did what she could to change her bandages and help with the healing process, but there was only so much she could do.

Mindy was barely talking, her sweet chipper personality had left her, she carried on being the mother she was born to be with Lucy, Eden, and Giselle, but she was lost without Alexa, her shine had left her.

All this combined made the driving painfully quiet. I tried to keep my eyes on the prize, although my sense of smell was clouded with the odor of bodies at times.

Missouri was no exception, we came across some human survivors, all headed to Manhattan, it seemed to be safe from the outbreak of werewolves—if you made it there.

Word was the army had blown up the bridges and anything swimming over was quickly taken care of by air support, the rooftops of buildings now housing mechanical birds—air force.

An outpost had been erected in Connecticut for survivors who would be flown over via a chopper.

As we traveled through, it became obvious that most of the werewolves inhibited their fears. And most backed off once they noticed us. A lot were stragglers who didn't want to pick a fight, likely wracked with guilt over whatever they had done. Still hungry enough to feel their human emotions. The ones who ran in gangs were made an example of if they attacked our truck. The blades became chipped from grinding thick bones, but there was enough rainfall still to wash off the blood stains from time to time.

The few times the fight did come to us, Evan was quick to deal with it, he never let me get in harm's way, and he was almost protecting me. He was a gifted fighter, street smart, but still, a lingering shadow of darkness followed him like a brand he'd never remove.

We got further north when I caught a few more familiar scents. Jax and Ezra were popping up loud and clear and they were less than two days away.

"Let's pull over for the night." I suggested.

Evan was sitting in the front of the truck with me, and we heard the girls chattering and headed round back.

"YES, I'm starving." Giselle grumbled.

"There's a good eatery in Indianapolis, we'll see what supplies they got left there and hopefully some food." I said.

"We should be looking for farms Arthur, there'll be livestock." Mindy disagreed with me.

She knew Evan and I would need to feed on more than pancakes and bacon even though I had never given into that carnal instinct, I had kept my diet completely normal. I just nourished myself with an abundance of meat, which we were lacking in.

"If a farm comes up, we'll stop, but I am not veering off track if we don't have to." I argued.

"Let us all starve then." she scowled.

"Get some sleep." I slammed the doors on the back of the truck and headed to the front to sleep in the cab.

I knew she was right; she was always right and what's worse is she knew it and she knew I'd be scolding myself for it, and here I was destined for the uncomfortable cab as my bed.

The door opened and it was Evan with two pillows in hand.

"You don't have to babysit me." I smiled with only one side of my lip.

"I'm not, I got kicked out too." he laughed as he handed me one of the pillows.

"Bloody women." I chuckled.

"She's just hungry, they all are." He sighed.

"I feel sorry for any werewolf who tries to attack tonight. Mindy would just as soon cook them up and eat'em." I joked.

"I hope not." Evan's face flushed white.

"Not you, not unless she wants a fight with Giselle." I winked.

"You caught that?" He smiled.

"It's pretty obvious." I smiled back.

Evan glared at me with a sarcastic expression.

"It's nothing." His grin deceived him.

"Maybe it should be." I pressed.

"We'll see, I've never had a girlfriend." He sighed.

"She's a nice girl, thick-skinned. She knows what you are... what's the worst that could happen?" I asked.

"The worst? I could eat her?" He chuckled half-heartedly.

"That's beyond you now. I don't think you would." I smiled trying to encourage him to have some faith in himself.

"I don't trust myself, Arthur..." He sighed.

"You should have a little more faith in yourself, Evan. Forget the doubt Graham raised you with and arm yourself with some confidence." I pressed.

"I want that, but I don't know how to be a different person." He slumped on his shoulders and buried his face in the pillow.

"You're already on the right path." I assured him as I squeezed his shoulder.

"You're a good man Art, I wish I had had a father more like you." Evan raised his head and leaned back into the headrest.

"Alexa would disagree." I sighed.

"She knew you guys were always on edge, I think she understood." Evan said.

"I was never there for her, not the way Mindy was. Tristan had more to do with her than I did. I was but a shadow of a presence." I said as I shut the mirror on the sunshade that glared back at me with a reflection I barely recognized.

"None of us had choices. She knew that." Evan said.

"There were choices, but staying was the easiest option. Going out on our own was dangerous at the time, even more so now." I felt like I was in a confessional as the words trickled out from my lips.

"Don't beat yourself up, you know where self-pity leads people like us." Evan plumped up his pillow and pressed it against the window, reclined his seat, and tried to find a comfortable position to sleep in.

"Get some rest big guy." I resonated with his desire to sleep and did the same.

An hour or so had passed when a bang against the window woke us.

"What was that?" I rubbed my eyes.

"Came from the roof." Evan was already awake and alert, his eyes trailing a new dent in the roof.

"The trees." I said with concern.

"Drive." Evan ordered as he opened the small, hatched window that led to the back of the truck.

"Lucy ran to the window from inside the truck screaming as the thuds on the roof became louder and louder. The roof of the truck began to slump inwards from the weight of the beasts that teased us with their presence, scrapping the metal roof just enough to make sounds akin to the likes of nails down a chalkboard.

"We've been followed." Mindy screamed as she picked up a loaded gun.

"Don't fire yet! We need the integrity of that roof to hold as long as possible." I yelled as I floored it down a dark highway.

As the truck raced faster through the empty roads the werewolves sunk their claws into the roof desperately clutching on for dear life.

"I'm going to see how many there are." Evan said as his hands changed, his teeth became sharp, long, and bloodied.

I nodded in agreement as I kept my eyes on the road.

"ARTHUR!" Mindy was screaming for me in the back as Evan tore the door off the passenger side of the truck and climbed up onto the roof.

"Hold on, honey!" I yelled back as I took a sharp turn trying to fling off anything, or anyone that shouldn't be there with jerky movements in my steering.

Evan let out a roar as he tossed a body into the road that bounced off the bonnet of the truck, quickly diced up by the blades.

The back door flung open, as I watched from the side mirrors. Eden began to scale the sides of the truck trying to climb onto the roof with a shotgun strapped to her back.

"GET BACK INSIDE!" I yelled as I slammed on the brakes.

The truck came to a sudden stop and the weight of the girls crashed into the cabin, three more wolves leaped over the blades and into the road. They were lit up with the truck's spotlights and Evan emerged. He skulked forward on all fours, as the three shuffled backwards acknowledging that Evan was far bigger than they were.

Eden crept forward and let off a round at one wolf and he dropped to the ground as a hole was blasted into his torso. His eyes fluttered between opened and closed and he dropped to the ground, still suspended by his hands as he fought through the pain and the way his body would heal him from what should be a fatal shot—at least to a human.

I climbed out of the truck and began to morph as the girls hopped out of the back armed with more guns.

"Just say when." Mindy said as she clung tightly to me even though my appearance was changing.

Eden was trigger-happy and moved herself in front of Evan as he snapped at them. I don't think she knew just how dangerous Evan was, even with all the control he had, if she got in his way, even *my* way, there's no stopping us.

"Arthur!" Lucy screamed as she turned around to notice another two werewolves on top of the truck.

One was too far gone, his eyes wild, somewhat bigger than the one next to him, more agitated and edgy, he licked his teeth as he made eyes at Eden.

"FIRE!" Mindy ordered and the girls began to let off rounds.

Evan was in the thick of it, he was fast and embodied pure devastation, his skills as a fighter and even more so a survivor shone brightly as he tore through two wolves of his similar size.

I leaped up to the roof and ripped the first wolf down giving Giselle a target to fire at, the backfire of the gun throwing her into Eden.

"Giselle!" Eden squealed.

The larger wolf hurled me off the side of the truck and I fell into a stump that impaled me.

I was stuck too far down on the stump to pull myself up and so the painful process of my body fighting and forcing the excelled healing began. I was still in eyesight of the fighting when Mindy raced to my aid, but she'd never get me off this stump — not alone.

"Stay down!" Mindy ordered.

Her eyes filled with worry as she guarded me with her two remaining rounds.

My hands now weapons, doubled in size rested on her forearm as I tried to show her some sort of human emotion. A part of me trying to tell her it was me inside and I was okay.

"You just stay down, I've got you." She rested her hand on mine as she traced the calloused nails where my fingers once were.

There was a loud scream from Eden. She was hurled onto the bonnet of the truck, she grasped desperately at the wiper blades trying not to fall into the blades.

"HELP!" she screamed.

The same werewolf who had been staring at her was stalking her now. Lucy and Giselle were too busy with the others to help her.

Mindy didn't hesitate; she walked along the side of the truck and fired a round into the beast's chest. It wasn't enough to take him out, but it would buy Eden some time.

"Get her down!" Mindy yelled.

Evan turned; he was covered in blood. Mostly from his own injuries but he had finally taken out the three wolves that stood in the road. Lucy and Giselle had taken out the small one but with great difficulty.

Evan leaped up on top of the truck, pulled Eden up onto the roof and saved her from falling between the blades.

He noticed I was missing and raced around the road searching before Mindy led the others to me.

He grabbed me and with one swift movement pulled me up and off the stump.

"Sit him up." Mindy ordered.

She knelt behind me, and she pulled out pieces of bark from my back.

"Stay as you are, you'll heal faster." she said as she walked away teary.

She always had a hard time seeing me like this, in the alternate body. It was a version of me she couldn't trust.

"Evan…" Giselle touched him cautiously.

He turned back into his human self, not trusting the werewolf around the girls alone. His human form exposed his wounds more obviously. He had wide-open gashes across his chest, a bite mark on his forehead reaching into his hair, and another set of claw marks that tore some muscle wide open on the back of his right leg.

"Oh my god." Giselle gasped as she walked around him to examine his injuries.

"Get them both into the back, we'll drive from now on." Lucy said as she looked to Eden to help her with me.

"I'm okay." Evan lied. The pain in his face was obvious.

"You don't need to be brave; you're missing half a leg." Giselle sighed.

"He's not going to eat us, right?" Eden asked Lucy as she approached me.

"I hope not." Lucy laughed as she winked at me.

Lucy knew I was one of the only wolves who had never fed on humans. There were only a handful of us who could say that.

"Come on." Lucy grabbed one side of me as she tried helplessly to hold me up, but in this body, at this size, it did little to help.

We waddled slowly to the back and Mindy climbed in with us to tend to our wounds with what supplies we had.

Giselle also joined us, leaving Lucy and Eden to drive the rest of the way.

"Head for Philadelphia." I shouted.

Mindy was cutting up an old blanket into long strips for her and Giselle to use as bandages. She leaned me forward and began wrapping the strips around me.

"Lay back and bite on this." I heard Giselle whisper to Evan.

She handed him an old strap and he bit down as she held up the torn flesh and held it back to his leg, he gasped out in pain as she tied it back into place with a ratchet strap to hold the muscle back in place.

"FUCK!" he yelled.

"I'm sorry." She apologized.

"We're not done, but I think that's the worst one." She sighed hesitantly.

She wet some strips with water as she cleaned off the dirt and old blood from his chest.

He watched her closely; out of fear or seduction, I wasn't sure anymore. But she was gentle as could be as she tied down a makeshift compound bandage onto his chest.

"That looks nasty." She stroked his forehead around the long deep gash.

"I have a headache." He held her wrist away from his face.

"I'll be gentle." She sat behind him with her legs crossed and pulled him back into her.

Her hair fell to the sides of her face and Evan relaxed as he leaned onto her legs.

"Will these heal?" She was curious.

"In a few hours, sometimes days or weeks. Depending on how bad the injury is, Arthur will be down for a few days." Evan explained.

"Evan's had the worst of it." Mindy teased proudly.

"Oh?" Giselle asked.

"Alexa hacked off my arm once." Evan sighed.

"Why?" Giselle asked curiously and her expression shifted.

"Evan wasn't always a good boy." Mindy scolded.

"I'm trying to be better." Evan replied.

Giselle smiled down as she stroked his cheek between cleaning the bite marks.

"I believe you." She whispered.

"Thank you." He held her hand to his cheek softly.

"Get some sleep Art." Mindy nodded as she wrapped herself in a blanket and threw Giselle and Evan some old sleeping bags.

Lucy and Eden were making good time while the rest of us slept as much as we could. They swapped between driving and sleeping. Taking it in shifts over the next two days.

I was able to walk around by this point, but in no state to take on another fight. Much like Evan, I was spent.

V.J.Garland

CHAPTER NINE

JAX

The journey down to Florida was surprisingly quick. We made it in one day and Liam was on the hunt for the closest fire station to the factory.

We found one three blocks away and Austin fueled the truck and as many jerry cans as he could find.

"We should take two, if something goes wrong with one, we're screwed." Austin pressed.

"I agree, at least if they both get there, we have double." I nodded.

"Well, there's three tankers here. The roads are quiet, we might do better taking all three." Liam smiled.

"Let's see if they all fill up." Austin nodded as he retrieved more cans.

This fire station is huge." I said as I looked around.

"Should we look around for supplies?" Austin asked.

"There's no time, we need to get the colloidal. Would have been handy if Celinde had come. I don't particularly feel like touching that stuff." I joked.

"We'll siphon it into the tanks somehow." Austin slapped my back.

"Let's get a move on." Liam said as he filled the last of the jerry cans.

We took a truck each and drove them over to the factory located the hoses in the truck and backed them up to a vat past a gated area stickered with warning labels and keep-out signs. There was more than colloidal back here, there was acid and all sorts of potentially dangerous chemicals.

"Okay, who's doing this?" Liam winced.

"Let's find some gloves, I don't feel like burning my face off." I shuddered.

"Good thinking!" Austin hunted through a safety shed and pulled out a thick pair of gloves.

"So, who wants to do the honors?" He held them in front of himself for one of us to grab them.

"I'll do it." Liam sucked in a breath regretfully.

"Good man." Austin smiled and helped him pull on the thick gloves.

"At least they're long." I shrugged.

"Let's do this." He growled as he punched the air in front of him and climbed the ladder on the vat with the free end of the hose over his shoulder.

He released the seal; it hissed as I sunk the hose into the drum created a seal with his thumb, pumped the liquid, and hurled the end to me as I tried not to spill any on myself as I dipped it deep into the tank.

"That was worse than your job!" I scowled as I brushed off a burn from my forearm.

"I don't think any of us are coming away without some sort of burn." Austin sighed.

"I don't think any of us are coming away from this at all." I said under my breath.

"You think so?" Liam asked.

"I think they stand a chance. But I don't think there's a place amongst humans for us anymore, and we don't fit alongside other werewolves either. With any luck, we'll take enough out that the humans can remove the rest. Maybe Celinde can find some peace finally." I confessed.

The tank began to ripple inside as it filled, and Liam hauled the hose to another truck.

It took almost half a day, but we had all three filled and there was still some if we needed it.

"Time to go." I ordered as we each climbed into a truck and sped north back towards Philadelphia.

As we traveled north, we came across signage. Not your usual signage. Warnings, bodies crucified on the sides of the roads. On the other side, a werewolf body is in the same position. Like declarations of war. We only stopped in open areas to fill the trucks. You could feel the tension in the air even without seeing a single body. The smell was putrid, it was the smell of rotting bodies.

"That's disgusting." Austin yawned as he tried to cover his mouth from the fumes as he fought through the exhaustion.

"Yeah, it's a little unsavory." I agreed as I coughed through the smell.

We'd been driving almost nonstop for nearly thirteen hours. I could see smoke in the far distance and knew it had to be Philadelphia. We were almost there.

V.J.Garland

CHAPTER TEN

CELINDE

I paced the halls anxiously, eyes always on me. Even though I felt safe here, there was something about this place, these people.

"I'm going to take a nap." I lied to Zane.

"I'll walk you up." He followed behind me.

This place oozed bad juju. Now that I'd eaten, I felt something a little more than hunger. My stomach did backflips every time I saw a staircase, every time Zeek came near me. He terrified me more than any werewolf could.

Zane was the only one I trusted. I trusted him because he didn't trust Zeek.

"Why do you protect me?" I asked as I pushed the door to our room open.

"You seem worth protecting." He answered.

"Zane…" I sighed.

He was silent as his jaw softened and he took me in.

"I don't want sex Celinde. Relax." He laughed.

"You possess secrets and Jax's trust. That's more valuable than gold right now." He sighed.

"What happens when it's not enough? Or if he shows up empty-handed?" I asked.

"We go to plan B." He replied.

"What's plan B?" I asked.

"There isn't one, not yet." He confessed and he went to lay down in his bed.

I lay in my nest awake for a while until I heard Zane snoring. It never took him long; he did that army thing where they taught you how to go to sleep in a minute. Once he was out, he was out for a good long while. It paid off to learn people's habits and I became an expert.

I slipped out of the room and up the back staircase.
Three flights up and I began to hear screaming, power tools, and what sounded like Zeek and Mateo fighting someone who sounded like they had been gagged.

I snuck up and peeked through the window of a door where I saw Zeek cutting through a young woman's leg. Her other leg was already amputated and the skin from it lay on the floor as Mateo deboned and wrapped it in saran wrap.

I almost gagged there and then. I quickly sprinted down the stairs as I realized how they seemed to have such a healthy supply of meat.

Zane stood in the stairway as I clumsily raced down.

"Shhh." He grabbed me and pulled me into the room.

"I didn't see anything." I whimpered.

"Yes, you did." Zane's expression hardened. "I don't like it either, and I don't eat it." He added.

"Why do you let them…" I blurted.

"My power in this place only has value as long as they are happy. I turn a blind eye." He sighed.

"You should too." He whispered as the stairwell opened.

"Go!" He pointed to our room as footsteps grew closer and I covered myself in the sheets to pretend I was asleep. As I hid, I heard the door open and Zane address Mateo.

"Has she been out?" He asked.

"No, she's been asleep the whole time." Zane replied.

"Were you?" He asked.

"Nah I was reading a book." Zane had a huge stack of books beside his bed. He wasn't the kind of guy I'd think was a reader, but it's not like he could exactly turn on the TV or go down to a bar and order wings while he watched the game.

"I could have sworn I heard someone upstairs." He grumbled.

"I thought you kept those doors locked?" Zane asked.

"We do..." He sighed.

"Maybe you're just paranoid considering the nature of what goes on up there." Zane said with a pang of judgment in his tone.

"I don't exactly like it either, but it's the last resort. The last hunt didn't bring back a lot of food. Not enough for all of us." He said.

"We'll get out of here as soon as we can." Zane said confidently.

"I'd like to put this chapter of my life behind me." Mateo agreed.

I heard trucks roll in, big trucks and I felt my soul leave my body for a split second as the sound was too familiar to anything about Christian.

My heart bled for him, in ways I didn't know I could feel pain and when I didn't feel pain, I felt nothing, a numbness. This was grief and I had no outlet. But grief was the final act of love. It was how my body reminded me it was real. How it screamed at me and punished me for letting someone love me so hard, for reciprocating that love and now there was a hole in the place I once had a heart.

Jax blew through the door, it was like he smelt my agonizing, and he was the only person I could grieve with because he was grieving the same losses. He nodded to Zane and Mateo, taking a second longer to inhale the scent of death Mateo wore.

He dropped to my level, and I peeled myself from the sheets.

"He's really gone..." I spluttered.

Jax was so somber but still graceful and pleasant as I wept into my hands. He reached for me and held my frailness as he wrapped me in a scratchy blanket.

"I'm sorry." He patted my back. "You and Carrie were always so strong for us." A tear escaped his eye, and I felt the weight of it hit my hair.

I had no words, I had sadness, aggression, and despair and I would never overcome any of it. I knew the world was evil now, it wasn't just werewolves doing horrible things. Humans were just as bad.

"Jax…" Liam called from the doorway.

They were preparing downstairs in the drop zone and needed our help.

"Let's take a raincheck on this crying stuff." I pulled back and wiped my eyes.

"You've been a sister to me Celinde, I will always be here for you." Jax assured me.

"Ditto." I forced a lip up to grin.

We all raced downstairs, and Lincoln met me with a packet of hardtack and instant coffee.

"Long night ahead." He smiled.

I smiled back as I grabbed the flask and biscuits and headed into the hot zone.

The sound of wolves grew closer, and I knew there was no backing down now. We would be surrounded in an hour.

"Here." Austin handed me a super soaker full of colloidal.

"Just like old times…" I huffed.

He brushed my hair back and pulled me in for a hug as he sensed my despair.

It wasn't the impending war on our doorstep that scared me. It was because I was facing this alone. Carrie was always beside me, *always*. But now I'd be alone. Liam, Jax, and Austin would be out there fighting, and I didn't trust my new community one bit now.

V.J.Garland

CHAPTER ELEVEN

LUCY

Eden was speeding and I strapped myself in a little tighter as we began to see a cityscape still covered with residual smoke not far from us.

"Watch out!" I screamed as a smaller poorly formed werewolf leaped at the truck and caught itself in the blades.

"Fuck!" She yelled.

"SPEED UP!" Giselle yelled from the back.

Eden pushed the truck to the best of its ability as she swerved between wolf after wolf. Even though they couldn't change entirely they still had more strength than a human.

"How much further Arthur?" I yelled.

"You're getting closer, not far now!" He assured me as he continued to writhe in pain.

By the time we reached a clearing before the city. The roof of the truck had been torn off completely and I screamed and yelled as much as I could to draw any sort of attention possible, hoping there could still be humans around in what was once a populated area.

I leaped from the truck and stood before a hoard of beasts as the truck slowed, they licked their teeth at my boldness. Most were still partially identifiable to their human selves. I cut at my arms with a pocketknife and let them sniff at my blood as it dripped to my fingers, it immediately offended them, and they slowly backed away. It was enough to get the truck to the hospital's uninviting gates where Liam and Austin tore at the chains to reach us as they called for more help. I was thrilled to see them, and it gave me hope Jax would be inside too.

Mindy and Liam helped Arthur inside and Austin helped Giselle with Evan. The looks shared between them were curious and I knew this may not be a warm welcome for Evan.

As soon as they were through the gates Austin dropped him to the ground and I rushed to help Giselle sit him up.

"You brought that animal here…" Austin spat at him as his teeth grew and he fought the urge to finish what was left of him.

"He saved our lives!" Arthur growled in Evan's defense.

Austin's jaw dropped and Jax appeared and pushed past him and Liam.

"Jax!" I threw my body at his and wrapped myself around him.

"Oh my god…" He held me tight and dropped the gun as he picked me up and kissed me.

"I didn't think you'd make it once I saw how bad it got." He whimpered with regret.

"No, I'm okay." I squeezed him tightly.

"Where's Lex?" Austin asked.

Mindy's face hardened and she refused eye contact with the others.

"Arthur?" Jax asked.

"She didn't make it son." He rubbed his eyes.

"MOTHERFUCKERS!" Austin was full of rage and began tearing through an old ambulance and nearly took out a few heads as he launched metal and wheels into various directions.

"Shit…" Jax placed me down as he went to Mindy's side trying to offer comfort.

"Don't touch me! You did this!" She slapped his face hard.

Jax backed away as he took the hit, and I felt the sadness wash over him as he slumped onto an old tire.

Mindy felt no remorse for her actions and kept close to Arthur with her head down.

"Who have we got here." A tall, bearded man approached with Celinde who looked worse than the last time I saw her.

"It's good to see you alive, Lucy." She hugged me.

I hugged her back and looked around at the faces of strangers.

"Where are the others?" I asked.

"We are all that's left." She whispered with sadness in the weight of her words.

"What do you mean *'we are all that's left'* Celinde?" Arthur growled.

"I mean we are all that's LEFT. Ezra, Christian, and Carrie are gone!" She screamed.

The bearded guy held her shoulder gently as if to hold her together and stop her from crumbling, she was clearly in a fragile state. She seemed to trust this man and gravitated towards him.

"What a fucking mess." Mindy said as she hugged Arthur.

They seemed to have this parental approach to the others. In the short time I had known them, they were always the ones I liked the most. Always willing to bend over backwards to help anyone with a no-judgment approach, even though their whole lives had been tipped upside down and shaken.

"You need help." He reached down to pull Arthur up, but he barred his fangs and pushed him away.

"More of you? Really?" He hissed at Celinde as he glared between Evan and Arthur.

They *can* be trusted, and they're hurt!" she scowled back.

"And you! What the fuck are you?" he glowered in my direction.

"I'm human…" I replied as I raised my hands in defense of myself.

"Why did those werewolves back away from you?" He demanded some sort of justification from me, and I noticed binoculars around his neck.

I pulled my hair back and removed my jacket which left me in nothing but a bra as I exposed my purple body.

Jax raced to my side and covered me up with his arms.

"What is that?" He asked but nobody was quick to answer.

"This is Zane, he has no manners." Celinde punched him in the arm, but he barely felt it.

"Zane, I was stuck in a well of some chemicals they don't seem to like. It stained my skin and it's in my bloodstream now." I replied.

The sky darkened and the howls of wolves were not far from the tree line. The fall of night was close, and they would be at their strongest. Capable of a full transformation, not a half-assed one like we'd seen from the crazed ones along the way.

"Colloidal silver, Jax and his guys just drove in three tanks." He smiled.

"That was generous of him." Mindy hissed.

"We're all fighting the same enemy Mindy." Jax pleaded with her.

"We don't have time for this, they weren't far behind us. They'll be here soon if they aren't already here waiting!" Giselle growled as she wiped old, browned blood off Evan.

"Can you fight?" Jax held his arm out to Evan.

Evan grabbed his arm and stood as best he could.

"I'll do what I can, but I don't think I'll be as lethal as I once was, not without feeding. Lucy on the other hand." He smiled at me kindly.

"Not a chance, she stays inside." Jax made himself clear even though I knew Zane and Evan were thinking the same thing.

"We'll fight from the walls with the first tank if they attack. If they get too close, we go over." Jax looked at Austin, Liam, Arthur, and Evan.

They didn't hesitate to agree with him.

"This place should have high-pressure hoses. We'd get a better reach without wastage." He said to a man in an apron.

"That's Lincoln, he's the cook." Celinde said softly as she took her place beside me.

"You look like you could use some rest." She whispered to me as Zane raced around looking for equipment with Lincoln and some other soldiers.

"They seem nice." I said as I rubbed my eyes.

"Don't be foolish, Lucy." Her eyes darkened at my words.

"Did they hurt you?" I asked.

"Not me…" Her words trailed off and I knew better than to press for more.

"I could use a rest if I'm being honest. I don't know how long I've been awake for now." I confessed to Celinde as my head dizzied at the thought of sleep.

"What about you two?" Celinde asked Eden and Giselle.

"Just until this heats up, I guess." Eden agreed.

"I'm going to stay with Evan, but thanks anyway." Giselle sighed as she leaned into Evan and held his hand.

Seeing her smitten with Evan was both heartwarming and a tragedy. I knew in my heart he'd be dead in hours if he didn't feed. It took all the strength he could muster to get out of the truck and now war was on our doorstep. He'd never make it.

We walked towards the building and Celinde took us in through the emergency room entrance and past a bunch of men who stunk of tobacco and whiskey.

"Is there any food?" I asked as I spied a door sign with the word kitchen displayed across it.

Celinde sighed as she pushed the doors open and rummaged through packets of opened and half-used MREs.

"There's some fresh kill in the fridge if you want to fry us all some meat." A seedy-looking man snickered in the doorway. His eyes bulged as he looked at Celinde with a gross feeling of intimidation. He looked me up and down and puckered his lips in my direction.

"I'd love a steak!" Eden was oblivious to the tension as she sucked down a tube of condensed milk.

"Sure, sweetheart!" He chuckled.

"Zeek…" Celinde was cautious with him as she said his name objectively.

"We should get some rest." I pulled at Eden as I took note of Celinde's discomfort around him.

"Suit yourselves. Plenty more where that came from." He grinned.

"I'm starving, I'll stay." Eden was still not looking at us and Celinde kicked her in the back of the shin, and she dropped to the ground.

"What the fuck was that for?" Eden wrangled her down to the ground in a headlock.

"Get off me!" Celinde struggled.

"STOP IT!" I pried them apart.

"Take your clothes off next time you're going to do that." Zeek licked a blade as he sliced steaks from a large chunk of meat.

"Here purple girl!" He hurled a slab at me. "Share it with GI Jane." He winked. The raw meat hit me in the face, and I caught it, and the blood quickly stained my hands.

Celinde slapped it from my hands and pulled a knife from a chopping block in defense when Jax walked into the commotion.

"What's going on?" Jax asked. Zane was behind him; the tension thickened.

Nobody answered. I gathered Eden and Celinde away from Zeek as Jax sniffed around and his eyes filled with rage.

"Do you know what this is?" He swiped at the bench and the slabs of meat went flying across the room.

"It's food, you should know that." Zeek taunted Jax.

"This is the kind of life you live?" Jax pressed a slab of the flesh into Zane's hands.

"Not all of us eat it." His expression was saddened.

"BUT YOU ALLOW IT!" Jax raged.

"Well, we can't exactly eat your kind. The meats too tough." Lincoln said as he approached the doorway.

"You're sick!" Celinde threw a chopping block at him. But he just laughed at her anger.

"Can we do this later? We've got wolves knocking at the door." Austin said too calmly.

"CELINDE, take the girls to a secure room." Jax growled.

"No, I'm helping." I argued.

"So am I." Eden pushed her way out of the kitchen before anyone could speak.

"You know I'm not hiding anymore…" Celinde sighed.

"Well fuck it then, you choose how you die!" Jax threw up his arms as he locked eyes with each of us as we defied his orders, he strolled outside and kicked a drum on the way out.

"You, I'll kill you before this is up." Celinde pointed a knife at Zeek.

He kissed the air and waved her off.

"Come on!" I pushed her outside. "He's not worth it." I added.

"I'm still throwing him over the fence…" she chuckled.

"You might not need to." I said as I pointed to Evan.

I knew Evan would heal faster if he was fed, but he hadn't fed on a human in years. An animal wouldn't quite cut it and we were fresh out of bears. There were plenty of werewolves, but we'd never get him back. That was too far. Zeek would be just enough.

"He's evil, what he's doing is evil." Celinde knew exactly what I meant, and we approached Giselle.

"Don't involve her… talk to me!" Evan demanded. He would have heard the whole thing.

"Zeek…. He's got some cannibal cafeteria going on." I sighed.

"He keeps them upstairs, I saw them. At least eight girls, some elderly." Celinde sighed.

"And you want me to kill him?" Evan asked.

"They are just biding their time out there. We are outnumbered. It would help you heal faster *and* remove the problem." Celinde whispered.

"If I do this, he'll never trust me again." Evan argued.

"If you don't, we'll all die anyway. So, all your efforts for respect and absolution will have been for nothing." I growled.

"Which one?" He grunted and let out a deep breath of regret.

"That one, do it quietly. We can't let his people know." I said as I pointed to Zeek.

"Bring him to me behind the garbage cans. Get Eden to do it." He ordered as he tried to stand.

"If this goes wrong..." Giselle started but her eyes quickly filled with tears, and she struggled as her sentence failed to leave her lips.

"I need you to know Gi, I might not be able to stop." Evan held her cheek as he pressed his forehead to hers.

Words failed her as she nodded, tears trickled down her face in one solid stream.

"If I had known you a hundred years ago, I'd have been different. I'd have been human for starters, but I'd have given you the world and life you deserved." He kissed her softly.

"It's okay, for now, for what we are living through. It was enough just to have someone feel what I felt." A tear dropped onto her shoe.

"I'm sorry, we don't have a lot of time." I urged as Zeek paraded through the grounds like he owned the place.

"Eden, get him around the back." Evan stood up shakily and walked off and I kept him in my eyes while Celinde held Giselle back. Giselle buried her face on Celinde's shoulder and wept.

"HEY! Zeek…" Eden hollered.

She waved him over to her as we tried not to look involved, and she walked alongside him towards the side of the building.

Giselle began to hyperventilate, and I sat her down trying to calm her.

"Giselle, please calm down!" I begged.

Jax heard her and he raced over with Zane.

"What happened?" Jax looked around. "Where's Evan?" He asked.

"He went for a walk." I lied and he knew right away that I was lying when we heard a loud growl.

"Evan…" Jax raced off to follow the sound of death and destruction.

Evan was fully turned now, his chest covered in blood and his eyes red as he feasted on Zeek. Eden ran to the safety of Jax and hid behind him.

"Evan?" Jax said with understanding and calm in his voice.

But Evan responded with a howl as he shot his eyes up into the air and swallowed down fingers and bones.

"Leave him, they're attacking!" Austin raced over to us.

"Guns!" Zane shouted as he passed us all guns.

We climbed ladders up to a platform where the watch towers were accessible and offered some amount of shelter.

"I need those hoses, Liam!" Jax looked around for him.

Liam and Lincoln had hoses attached to one of the trucks and explosives wired to another.

"You know I might have to do the unthinkable..." Jax whispered as he pulled me aside in the shelter and pressed me against a wall, his nose touching mine as he closed his eyes hard.

"The cannon beach thing?" I knew what he meant from the stories he had told me and the dull tone in his voice.

"Yeah—if that happens you need to get out of here." He sighed.

"Turn them!" Mindy climbed the ladder below us. "Make them yours, you're good at that!" She sighed as she forgivingly hugged him.

"You are a born leader, my boy. All you need is for them to see it." She had a plan, and it was smart.

"Lead them away." I kissed him longingly. I knew I'd never feel his touch again and I drank in everything about him like it was the last drop of beer after a long week of study— but one thousand times harder.

"It's what Christian would have done." Celinde agreed.

Liam was spraying the hose as wolves attempted to climb the perimeter. Some got through and Liam was the first to turn, he was the most identifiable in his other form. He fought wolves smaller than him as they danced in puddles of blood fighting back one after the other. There were too many though and Jax gave me that regretful look.

"I gotta help him." He said over the howls and gunfire.

"I know." I took one last glance at Jax as he sprung out of the shelter.

I watched as he let himself change. Blood trickled from his claws, and I heard his bones snapping loudly and other werewolves froze as they looked on in horror, their eyes bulging as they took in his size. Some backed away into the tree line, others simply froze, but more became aggressive with fear.

Jax leapt down from the fence and into the hoard of werewolves and one after another they tried to take him down. His swipes and knocks took them out with ease. But he was too outnumbered. Evan was on the wall now with Liam defending the towers and Zane's crew had now emptied a whole tank.

"HOOK UP THE OTHER ONE!" Zane yelled at Lincoln.

"Don't shoot them!" I yelled.

I snatched the hose from Zane, I didn't trust him not to shoot Jax and I aimed it further away from where he was.

"You're going to need more than this." Mindy yelled as she hauled a long hose to another wall that they had begun to climb, and Arthur followed after her.

"Celinde! What do they have in the kitchen?" I yelled out to her.

"Can openers, some cleavers." She shouted over the noise.

"Giselle, get the knives!" I ordered and I tore off my jacket and armed myself with a gun filled to the brim with colloidal.

"What are you doing Lucy." Celinde grasped my wrist.

"Nothing…YET." I whispered. "You know I can't tell you anything without it being heard, just trust me." I added.

"I hope you know what you're doing…" Celinde released me moved towards Zane and helped with loading homemade grenades with the liquid.

V. J. Garland

Chapter Twelve

MINDY

There was blood everywhere on the scaffolding where we all stood as we tried to defend the hospital grounds.

Jax was trying with all his might to keep the walls clear but was injured beyond being able to regenerate before another injury occurred.

"Evan, help him!" I growled in his direction as he tore into another beast.

His eyes were red and darkening as he consumed my words, we shared a look of understanding between wolf and woman. He leapt into the mass of werewolves and landed a few feet away from Jax where he was almost covered from head to toe in bloody injuries. Evan tore wolves from him and Jax let out a loud growl. But it wasn't one of defeat, it wasn't pain, it was a piercing howl. One I had never heard from any of our men. Jax's eyes glowed as he rose in size, and he flexed his jaw. This was it.

"Hold the hoses." I yelled as I looked into the masses.

Wolves circled Jax but he went after the largest ones, and he showed no mercy now as he ravished the bodies with a hunger he hadn't nourished in years. His eyes were immediately red as he gorged himself on body after body and tore through any wolf who attempted to copy or attack him.

Liam and Austin jumped over the wall next as more wolves began to try and fight against him and Evan.

"Don't you dare leave me Arthur!" I gripped his shirt as I pulled him back away from the ledge.

"Oh, my darling. This is the end of the line." He brushed tears back from my cheeks.

"NO, it isn't. You have never been like that! You don't have to do this!" I wailed. "You can't leave me alone without Alexa. Now you!" I screamed.

Lucy and Celinde pulled me back as Arthur's gums bled and his eyes burst a yellow hue and his veins swelled as I watched him grow in size right before my eyes.

"I'm sorry." He blew me a kiss through his claws, leapt into the pack, and immediately followed Jax's lead feasting on wolf after wolf.

"Now what?" Celinde yelled.

"Trust the process." Lucy was like a zombie as she watched on.

The wolves had stopped trying to attack us, they were fixated on Jax and his gargantuan size. And his small army that defended his might.

Jax froze and so did everything else that could take a breath. He walked amongst his own kind, his muzzle the same red as his eyes. There wasn't an inch of him that wasn't drenched in blood now and his wounds healed before our eyes with speed. As he walked, he commanded obedience and most of the rouge wolves bowed to him, those that didn't were quickly dealt with.

"Fuck! Now what?" Zane said in a panic.

Celinde looked at me as Jax, Evan, Arthur and the others finished off any werewolf that wasn't in allegiance with them.

It was the largest pack we'd ever seen and soon Jax's attention was on us as he licked his teeth and sunk his claws into the shoulder of a smaller werewolf and quickly tasted the blood as he scanned the walls. He had a new target.

They were a few hundred feet from the wall now and Lucy scaled her way down on a rope and cut off the length, isolating herself away from us.

"What are you doing!" Celinde growled.

"Throw me the hose." She ignored Celinde as Jax slowly skulked his way back to the wall.

Zane hurled grenades into the darkness as Celinde lowered the last hose down to Lucy.

"I hope you know what you're doing!" I yelled.

She aimed the hose into the crowd that grew closer every second, but she moved forward for every wolf she took out and watched mystified as they curled up in pain.

"JAX, PLEASE STOP!" She screamed in fear.

But he wasn't himself anymore and he hadn't been for years.

"Get out of there!" Lincoln yelled as Mateo jumped down excitable and not ready to let Lucy take the reins.

Evan leapt at Mateo. He'd already tasted his cannibalistic friend and had been edging for more since the attack. He took his time with Mateo. Jax stalked around Lucy as she tried to speak to him helplessly. He was playing with her.

"Jax, you can get through this..." She was shaking with fear as she bent the hose preventing it from harming him, but he didn't care.

He stood taller now, over ten feet, and horrifying. Teeth the size of a finger and claws sharper than obsidian.

She aimed the hose and loosened the fold, but Liam threw himself in front of Jax and began to squirm in pain. Jax stepped over the top of Liam with no remorse as he forced Lucy back into the wall and she tore a knife across her wrist and flicked the blood at him. He flinched at the burn but kept moving forward.

"Fuck, it's empty." I whispered to Celinde.

"Well, it was nice knowing you." I slumped in defeat to my knees as I watched over the wooden planks.

Lucy's scream echoed loudly as Jax sunk his teeth into her neck. The deeper he mauled the weaker he became, and his face glistened in a silver hue as he dropped her body, and he became smaller and sunk to her level.

I could only put it down to his size and strength to be what kept him alive for so long after ingesting the poison. I saw him one last time before his skin ignited into acidic burns and flames. Lucy was still in his arms lifeless.

"Wait…" Giselle yelled.

Evan was running towards the wall when he dropped to the ground and the life left his body. Austin and Liam were next, they sat together in the red grass as if they were ready for this moment.

Hunter's Moon: Caged

V.J.Garland

CHAPTER THIRTEEN

ZANE

Arthur made it up the wall and Celinde raced over to Mindy, and she held onto them, and Arthur fell to his knees and let nature take its course as his body shrunk and shriveled into an ash cloud.

Celinde and Mindy soon followed, they went differently. They weren't like ash blowing in the wind, they just disappeared like smoke.

"Fuck!" Giselle kicked the planks and hurled things over the edge as every werewolf in sight exploded into a violent death of their own.

The hours had passed by quickly. It was almost dawn now and the bodies were all gone, they vanished as if they had never existed. The only trace left behind was the gore of the blood that rained last night.

I've seen a lot of horror in my life, but nothing compared to this. Nothing compared to the way Lucy sacrificed her life to spare the rest of us. She knew Celinde knew, and Mindy knew what she was going to do, and it was the bravest and most devasting act I've seen in my life.

The months following the Philadelphia attack were quiet. The odd straggler would come out, but we knew how to beat them back now.

The worst of it was over, and the best of them were at rest.

The End.

Hunter's Moon: Caged

V.J.Garland

Hunter's Moon: Caged

V.J.Garland